BLUE FATE 1
STARTUP

CASS TELL

BLUE FATE 1
STARTUP

A novel from the Blue Fate series

destinēe media

CHAPTER 1

For weeks I'd been gazing out at the churning surf wondering if TechZip would survive but today my thoughts were all about Janie. She said she'd be here. Didn't happen.

I kept telling myself not to think anything of it, but because of last night and the telephone calls this morning it made me worried. That filled me and made me oblivious to the life around, the kids running and digging in the sand, teenagers trying to dunk each other under the water, balls and Frisbees flying. While my eyes constantly scanned the people in the water, somehow their movements were a blur, as I felt like a suffering addict obsessed by her.

A few hours ago I'd tried to call Janie on her cell phone and was surprised when a male voice answered.

"May I talk to Janie?" I asked.

"Who is it?"

"It's Hank. Did I call the right number?"

"Get lost."

The line went dead and that rattled me. I carefully redialed her number and called again.

"Yeah?" It was the male voice.

"I want to speak with Janie."

"Listen, don't call back." The voice was deep and husky and something about it sounded east coast.

"What's going on? Is this her uncle?" I asked.

"No, but let me give yuh a word of advice. Drift away, if you get my point."

"What are you talking about? Who are you?"

"Listen kid, Malibu is off limits and don't even think about coming by the house."

"I want to talk with her."

"She ain't there and don't wanna talk to you. Like I say, get lost." He hung up.

From that point on my mind was racing. There was no way that Janie wouldn't want to talk to me, totally inconsistent with the way she expressed herself last night... except maybe there was a reason.

Last night we crossed a boundary that took us deep into each other's souls. I knew from experience it's the one thing in a relationship that introduces a new set of complexities. Maybe she had lover's regret, all those second thoughts that rush in the day after, and therefore the rejection. Not what I needed. Rejection touches my deepest being like a heavy history.

I was angry with the guy on the phone. He told me to get lost. Yeah, right. Who the hell was he anyway?

I thought back to our departing words last night, somewhere around three in the morning. When we walked out to her car she looked at me mischievously and gave me a long deep kiss and said, "I'll see you tomorrow at the beach." Then she got into her hundred thousand dollar sports car, and yelled out, "Love yuh Hank," and sped off down the street.

Impulsively I waved and yelled back, "I love you too."

And that had surprised me. Those were words I'd never said to anyone before, and I mean anyone. Growing up I didn't get much love, and the whole concept was foreign and difficult for me to deal with. When I thought about it after she left, and then all day today, I questioned if it was true. What is love anyway?

But, I can't remember ever feeling like that toward any other girl. The fact is, she had gotten under my skin and rocked something in the core of my being, and it had all happened so fast. Way too fast. The only negative thing was that she had slowed down my project, TechZip, a startup company that I had worked so hard to launch. The question that has been driving me for so long is whether my unique idea could become a successful business, but she has derailed me.

To be with her supersedes everything else.

All day I sat there in the lifeguard chair facing out at the blue Pacific, my eyes scanning the waves, watching swimmers, trying to be attentive to their movements, but I constantly kept glancing back at the empty space in the smooth sand where I first saw her lying on her pink towel… the tiny bikini. I just couldn't stop myself from looking for her, and anyway I was experienced enough as a lifeguard to handle any problem.

In the six years I'd been doing this I pulled a lot of people out of the water. People drowned, but never on my watch. It sickened my stomach to think about it.

Actually, most of the time the job is pretty boring. It might even seem like we are getting paid to kill time, but lives are at stake. Besides watching people in the water, we have other responsibilities, like sometimes we have to ask people to settle down when they get too rowdy, to not drink alcohol on the beach and abide by the rules. That's not too often.

A couple of weeks ago there were three drunken bikers down here that provoked a fight with some college students, and I intervened, and the bikers turned on me and it got rough for a bit. When the police got here it was all under control, although one biker needed some medical treatment. But it was quickly forgotten, about as much time as it took for the blood to dry and get turned under the sand. Things like that are exceptions. I'm not concerned about those guys, but worry for what I am.

For me, like many of the other lifeguards, this is a summer job to raise some cash. It helped pay my way through university and fund my project. Of course Janie had set me on a new course and this morning I was wondering where we would take our relationship from here? My job was coming to an end in two weeks and I had planned to get back to my project full time. Janie said she was heading back to school on the east coast. But I didn't want it to be just a summer fling. That phone call had put everything into a spin.

I tried to quit thinking of her and concentrate on the job. I scanned across the people and body of water in front of me. Rough surf today, some undertows. I glanced behind me. Would she come like she said?

I dwelled on the male voice on her cell phone and wondered if she was seeing another guy, perhaps someone from her social group? Not like me. In fact, she had mentioned a boyfriend who was still in the picture.

Then something jarred me from my thoughts when I heard a scream and my attention quickly shifted away from Janie and I saw a woman in a blue one piece swim suit running toward the water. Beyond her out in a calm spot between two sets of oncoming breakers was a boy maybe seven or eight years old, out too far, floundering, arms thrashing, fighting to keep his head above the water.

Immediately I knew it was stupid to be daydreaming like that, and my instincts took over. I grabbed the lifeguard-buoy and sprinted to the edge of the dry sand, and then with a few long strides was in the water knee deep, and dove and began to swim. I powered through the surf, long strokes pulling me forward, but when someone is in trouble, you feel like a barge when you want to be a speedboat. My eyes were on the boy and he fought to stay up as a large crashing breaker whipped over his head and then it passed and he disappeared.

It was an eternity to get to the spot where he went under and I got there and plunged beneath the surface, opened my eyes, and in the blur of sand and surf I saw his red swimsuit. I went to him and wrapped an arm around his chest and pushed off the bottom and made it to the surface, pulling the boy's head into the air.

"You okay?" I blurted, my eyes burning from the salt water.

He didn't answer and I quickly saw he was unconscious and wasn't breathing. My heart began to pound and I said to myself come-on, come-on, this can't be true. Quickly I headed toward the shore, my right arm wrapped around the boy's chest, using a sidestroke with my left arm, and my legs kicking as fast as I could. I reached a place where I could stand and held the boy in my arms and began to run through the water feeling like each step was slow motion.

When we got to dry sand I hurriedly placed the boy on his back and turned his head to the side and checked to see that his tongue wasn't swallowed. He still wasn't breathing, cold flesh, but I thought I felt a heart beat. I wasn't sure. I kneeled astride his knees and with my hands on top of each other pressed against his upper abdomen just below the rib cage.

Water flowed from his mouth and I pushed several more times to clear the water from his lungs and esophagus.

He still wasn't breathing. Come-on, come-on, please God, this can't be happening. Stay cool.

The woman in the blue swimsuit was screaming, "My baby, my baby. No, please no-o-o-o!"

A crowd was gathering around us.

I knew I only had four to six minutes before there was brain damage, even less adding in the time it took to get him out of the water. I put my finger on his neck and felt his carotid artery and sensed a slight pulse and quickly put my lips to his, pinched his nose, exhaled and made him take four deep breaths.

Then the boy made a small cough, and then coughed deeper, and again, and then vomited some salt water. Oh God, thank you.

The woman sobbed. "Is he going to be alright?"

I replied, "Yes, but we'll need to get him to the hospital to have him examined. Does anyone have a cell phone?" Mine was back at the lifeguard stand.

Someone had a cell phone and handed it to me and I called our emergency lifeguard rescue number and gave them instructions.

The boy whimpered and his body started to shake.

A crowd of people gathered around us. Just behind the mother was a guy wearing a pink and green Hawaiian shirt and black slacks. He yelled at me, "Why'd you take so long? The kid was right there in front a yuh going under and yuh just sat there on yur ass." He had a broad chest and looked to be about forty-five.

Standing next to him was a bald guy with a thick neck and large muscular arms. He was wearing black leather shoes, brown pants and a dark blue short-sleeved shirt. He reminded me of a professional wrestler. He stared straight at me with dark eyes and spoke loudly so everyone could hear, "Yeah, shows this guy's a lazy bum. The kid could-a died."

CHAPTER 2

I couldn't wait for the day to end, feeling like crap because of what happened to that kid and wondering if I could have done anything better, especially after what those two guys had said about me. And Janie was still on my mind.

In thinking about her I knew she lived not far away and a plan came to my mind.

At five o'clock my shift ended and I walked away from the lifeguard stand, got into my fifteen year old jeep and drove from Point Dume State Beach over to the Pacific Coast Highway. I headed south for a couple of miles and parked close to the turn-in to Paradise Cove Road. Paradise Cove is an area where a number of well-known movie stars live and some lesser-known people who are richer than the movie stars.

About a mile down the road at Paradise Cove is a small pier and a café. It's a place where a number of movies have been filmed. The parking is expensive down there, but that wasn't my concern right now.

I walked down the road a bit and then traversed south along the side of a hill through some brush until I could get a view of Janie's family's place. I wanted to see if her car was there.

Her family has a five-acre beach estate about a quarter of a mile south of the pier. It consists of a hacienda style house on a bluff above the ocean. Besides having five bedrooms and five bathrooms, the house has a gigantic living room with large windows and a magnificent view of the Pacific Ocean.

Their land slopes down a hill and a golf cart path leads to a Spanish style structure strategically designed with a view of the ocean, but also with immediate access to a tennis court, swimming pool and large manicured lawn with a putting green on the far side. This was where they entertain guests and have parties. From there the property drops down another level where there is a guesthouse close to the sandy beach. The guesthouse looks to be at least three or four times bigger than any house I've ever lived in.

An access road leads into their property and ends at a parking area where there is an eight-car garage next to the main house. Trees and hedges rim the property as well as a wire fence with state of the art surveillance equipment.

Yesterday Janie invited me to see the place and we had lunch and we swam in the pool. She told me this is their summerhouse, where her uncles sometimes stay when they come to Los Angeles on business. She stays in the guesthouse when she comes out here. She didn't take me down there.

Now my primary objective was to find Janie and see if I could talk to her. I didn't see her car in the parking lot, which was empty. Her car is easy to spot, a red Ferrari, a gift from an uncle. She said one of her uncles gave a speech at her birthday party down there on the property attended by a select group of his business associates. He had joked, "It's a little something she can drive around when she comes out to California," Janie told me that the real reason for the gift was that it represented a status symbol, something to impress the business associates. She said she gladly took the car, but then found out that it created ogles and stares from people, and strange men hitting on her that she could live without.

The grounds looked empty except for a gardener who was trimming bushes near the lawn, and there was a man sitting back under the shade of the lawn house. He was far away and in the shadows and I could only see that he was wearing dark pants. I wished I had my binoculars with me, but they were back at my apartment.

Janie told me that security people watched the house, so I suspected that the guy down there might be some kind of a guard.

I took out my cell phone and tried to call Janie again but the line just beeped. I considered to try and go onto the property and look around, but decided against it. All I needed was to get arrested for illegal trespassing. The last time I was arrested was when I was fifteen, but since then, for the past thirteen years, I've had a clean record. Of course I'm not counting that other thing that happened when I was in the Marines. In fact, I'm not even sure it's on my official records. But, all it takes is one new arrest and the police will dig up all that stuff from the past and it's held against you by the judge, so I had to be careful.

In not seeing her car I gave up my search and made my way back to my car and drove to my place in Venice Beach, about twenty miles south of Malibu and Paradise Cove. I live in a small apartment, if you can even call it that. It's basically a room above a garage that's connected to a run-down house three blocks away from the beach.

I turned in from the main street into a small alley and then drove through an opening in a high wooden fence into the back yard, onto an area of hard packed dirt, sand and weeds. Because Venice Beach is a popular place to visit, it's always difficult to find a place to park. Therefore, a couple of years ago some of the renters here knocked a hole in the fence and we now have our own private parking lot.

The room above the garage has been my home for seven years. Other people live in the main house connected to the garage and sometimes it's hard to tell exactly who the renters are with so many different people coming and going. The owner doesn't really care as long as the rent gets paid. A year ago I started to rent the garage below my place so that I could have more space to work on my startup company, TechZip. That's where I worked out the initial prototype and the patent application, but now Campbell Labs over in Culver City is helping with further design and production work.

When I first moved in here a local band used the garage every night for practice and on weekends they moved their equipment out into the dirt yard and it became a place to party. It came to a point where I couldn't study, so I put a stop to the parties down there. It caused a fight, but it didn't last long. The parties now take place in the house and are much more subdued affairs.

Obviously my intervention didn't make me popular around here for a while, but after a few months a new group of people were living in the house and they didn't know a thing about the back yard parties. But because of the fight, somehow my reputation expanded way beyond proportion and was now something like "don't mess with him; he's this crazy ex-Marine who lives above the garage". I even heard one pothead say "he's this hyper crazy ex-Marine who fought his way out of enemy territory with only a knife and he slit the throats of a hundred people in order to escape". And, when they're really high the story goes something like, "he's this psycho ex-Marine only comes out at night and stalks the streets of L.A., like a Rambo type vigilante hunter".

Each new group seems to have added something new to the story so that by now I have become some kind of urban legend. They didn't know that my going out at night was to jog along the beach, or to workout at a twenty-four hour gym.

Anyway, that reputation suits me just fine as it gives me considerable leverage whenever I need to negotiate anything with any of the transient residents in the house. In actuality, as a Marine I never made it into any war zones and spent my entire two years at Camp Pendleton about eighty miles south of central L.A. They don't need to know that.

★ ★ ★

I got out of my jeep and walked up the set of wooden stairs on the side of the garage each step creaking, and opened the three locks on the door. Shortly after I moved here I put a security door in place after some stoned partygoers kicked down my door and looked for food when I wasn't there. They went away hungry.

I opened the door and walked inside and stood for a moment thinking of last night. My place consists of one room, with a tiny kitchen and kitchen-bar on one side and a single bed on the other. A door leads to a small bathroom. Against one wall is a long table with stacks of books and papers all related to my business project. A bookshelf holds all my books from university. The walls are covered with an assortment of papers with hand drawn diagrams and flowcharts. A couple of mismatching chairs are randomly placed in the room.

A well attended-to green houseplant is on a stand over in the corner and on the wall above it is a reproduction of a painting, *The Angelus* by Jean-François Millet. It is of a young man and a young woman standing in a field at the end of the day, their heads bowed, praying. The sun has set, a golden glow is on the horizon where one sees the church tower, and a spiritual feeling radiates from the painting. It is the only religious artifact I have in the place, except for a Bible on my bookshelf given to me by Rochelle when I was sixteen. Sometimes at the end of a hard day of work I look at the painting and it gives me peace. The original hangs in the Orsay Museum in Paris and I'd love to go there some day to see all the art. In fact, if I could make a little money from my project I'd go see all the big art museums in Europe.

On one table close to my bed there is a small framed picture of a young sixteen-year-old girl, frail, smiling, looking down at a small baby held in her arms. Next to it is a vase with some daisies. I try and change the flowers every week. That photo stirs up all kinds of thoughts and emotions in me. It's my mother holding me, the only photo I have of her, taken when she still looked young and innocent, before the drugs ate up her youth and took away her life. Obviously I didn't get my genes from her, but from my father who was probably built like an NFL linebacker.

A quick feeling of nostalgia hit me, but not only because of the photo. This is where Janie and I were last night. I could never figure it out, but for some reason she had insisted on coming here. It embarrassed me, especially knowing where she lived.

This had been home for me for seven years ever since I got out of the Marines. The rent is exceptionally cheap and that enabled me to get through six years at UCLA and now one year into my project. It is not the kind of place where I willingly bring people. Why Janie had wanted to come here was a mystery. In fact, last night when she came here she said the place was like a refuge, not ordered and directed when compared to her life. I couldn't figure that out. I'd trade her place for mine any day of the week.

I went in, undressed, took a shower and put on a pair of clean shorts. I opened the fridge and scanned the contents; a couple of cans of beer, a half empty bottle of ketchup, some sliced cheese with a red 'discount' label on the package, and a bowl of spaghetti. I couldn't remember how long the spaghetti had been there, maybe four or five days, for sure longer than the time I'd known Janie.

I poked at the spaghetti and it felt like cold rubber. After heating it in the microwave I sat at the bar, poured ketchup on it and ate in somber quietness. When finished I rinsed off the bowl and then took some work related papers off the table and went to the bed, arranged some cushions and leaned back in a reclining position.

I tried to read, but couldn't concentrate, feeling tired because I hadn't slept much lately, and the emotions of the day were dragging me down. Remembering Janie's presence on the bed last night made me feel uneasy, like a lingering sense of perfume. I made another attempt to call her, but her phone had a busy signal and it didn't switch into her voicemail.

My thoughts went back though the day and I was still angry at what the male voice had said, trying to remember his exact words. The more I thought about it, the more I was convinced he had a New York accent, or from somewhere back there. That's where Janie lived most of the year, so all kinds of ideas were going on in my head, trying to look at it from every angle, and then I began to have some doubts and wondered if she had really been honest with me since we met.

Was that her boyfriend from back east who answered the cell phone, the lawyer she mentioned? Had I just been a summer fling for her? Or, had I done something to hurt her last night?

Well, so what, I thought. I've been rejected before. In fact, rejection has been a part of my entire life and I've learned to live with it. First of all going from home to home when I was growing up, and that combined with a string of dysfunctional relationships with girls in high school and as an undergraduate at UCLA. My best friend Jake sadly joked about this, how we always ended up being losers when it came to girls.

Clyde and Rochelle, our foster parents when we were teenagers, have spent a lot of time with us trying to help us understand our perceptions of the world, and why we make certain choices. Rochelle should know. She's a psychologist working part time for the L.A. County Hospital and then with the county social services. She says that Jake and I are typical of many foster kids. We suffered a lot of hurt and rejection and somehow that's all we know, and the people who hurt us can actually become our role models. We emulate their behavior.

But, no matter how much you consciously know it, Jake and I seem to always make bad choices, especially when it comes to girls. Jake said it was like wading into the La Brea Tar Pits where you slowly get submerged into deep relational ooze, almost suffocating, and somehow you manage to get out, only to step back in again.

Rochelle is tough with us but always positive. She says that things can be different; that we don't need to repeat the past and that it's possible to find love. Fat chance. A year and a half ago Jake got married and it lasted less than four months. He married Martha, this wild thing that was sleeping around from day one. That experience just about broke him. He was in the same MBA program as me, but he dropped out a few classes shy of graduating, slept on my floor for a few months, and is now a short order cook at Sloppy Sam's Hamburger Heaven over near Wilshire Boulevard.

Rochelle always tells us that we are looking for love in the wrong places and to meet nice girls we should go to church. In fact, I stopped going to church when I left Clyde and Rochelle to go into the Marines.

But before that, during the three and a half years I lived with them, we went to the South Central Baptist church every Sunday. It was true that there were some nice girls there, but Jake and I were in a minority and there was this kind of unspoken divide.

After high school I joined the U.S. Marines for two years, and after that went to UCLA. I went through several bad relationships during that time, so when I got the MBA I decided to avoid women and fully devote myself to my business plan. Then I ran into cash-flow problems, and went back to the lifeguard job, and Janie came along and knocked me over like a hurricane.

Maybe I just need to do what the male voice said, to "drift away". Maybe it's time to refocus on TechZip, but getting over someone like Janie won't be that easy. She crawled deep into my head, or maybe it's more like I sunk into the deep relational ooze.

I lay back on the pillow and tried to think it through. Should I pursue Janie, or just cut my losses and run? The attitude of the guy on the phone only made it worse and I felt like pounding his head against a wall, something I'm good at, which is difficult to admit.

CHAPTER 3

With my head on the pillow I kept thinking of the previous three days, what happened and why things went wrong. Three days isn't much time, but guys like me fall real fast, real hard. Is it love or obsession?

I didn't want the lifeguard job but it was out of necessity. Last Spring my project had not advanced as expected and the bank account had dropped to zero. So, a couple of months ago I drove over to the L.A. County Lifeguard office in Santa Monica where I had worked the previous summers. All the jobs were taken, but I got lucky. Just that morning a position had been freed up in Malibu, so I jumped on it, and while it was a pain to drive the twenty miles there and back every day, I was grateful for the job. My plan was to make it through the summer, build up a cash reserve and then get back to the project full time.

Malibu was different than Santa Monica, being somewhat isolated from the rest of Los Angeles. In the summer months Santa Monica had huge crowds of people pouring in from L.A. Malibu is different where there is a large local crowd, everybody knowing everyone else. It also has a different class of people. The houses in Malibu are exorbitantly expensive and people have money. It's kind-of weird for me to be around people like that.

So, three days ago, about an hour before ending my shift in the early afternoon I was thinking about my business plan when I heard some noise over at the volleyball courts behind me to the right. I turned and saw Mike greeting a girl who was walking onto the sand carrying a pink beach bag. He laughed and said, "Hay Janie. Where's the party?" Mike is a local beach bum who spends every day of his life playing volleyball and talking with the girls. Every night he can be found at local parties in Malibu and Santa Monica. Once he invited me to a party at his place where it seemed like he consumed a hundred cans of beer. All beaches in California have guys like Mike.

Janie, the girl he was talking with, had long blond hair and was wearing dark sunglasses and a very small green bikini, just covering the essentials. She had a body like you wouldn't believe. And, then she gazed over at me, saw me looking at her and she just stared me in the eyes. She held her look intently and it was like one of those impressions where you wondered if you had met before. It made me uneasy and I quickly turned back toward the ocean where my eyes should have been focused in the first place.

The next time I turned around I saw she has moved to an empty spot just off to the side of my lifeguard stand where she placed her pink beach towel. She was sitting on the towel and spreading sun cream over her long legs, then her stomach, her shoulders and and then the upper part of her breasts. Her hands moved like a deliberate dance, slow and sensual. And then she took a book from her pink beach bag, rolled over on her stomach and began to read.

It gave me a chance to check her out. The bottom of the bikini was small, almost a string. Her waist was slim and her long back had muscle tone. After some minutes she flipped over onto her back and held the book up in the air with two hands and continued to read.

I checked her out again. She had creamy light skin and didn't look like someone who spent hours in the sun. After fifteen minutes or so she put her book back into her bag got up, folded up her towel and then looked up at me. And she smiled.

That churned my stomach. I smiled back.

She walked away, but her image stayed in my mind.

★ ★ ★

That day my shift ended and I headed for my car. I needed to get to Culver City where I had scheduled a late afternoon meeting with Robert Campbell.

As I approached my car a voice behind me said, "Hey lifeguard."

I turned. It was her. She had put on a pink t-shirt with 'Vassar' printed on the front. The t-shirt ended just below the bottom of her bikini, her long slender legs seeming to extend to China. She carried the pink beach bag over her shoulder.

Before I could say anything she asked, "How long have you been a lifeguard?"

"Ah… six summers," I responded. Her sunglasses were resting on her head and I saw that her eyes were this extraordinary gray-blue.

"So what do you do during the winters?" she asked.

"I'm, ah, working on a project, trying to start a company." I wondered why she had followed me here, and why the interest, but I sure didn't object. "Uh, how about you?" I pointed at the writing on her t-shirt, but then realized I was probably rude. Quickly I said, "Vassar."

She nodded and ran her hand across the writing, her fingers delicately flowing across her breasts. "I live on the east coast and go to school at Vassar."

"How's that?" I asked, my eyes fixed on her shirt. "I mean, what are you doing in Malibu?"

"My family usually comes out here every summer. We have a house just south of here."

"Sounds tough." I grinned.

She smiled, but her eyes seemed sad and she looked down. "More than you know." She wiped some sand from her forearm and said, "I'm thirsty. Would you like to join me for a lemonade?"

"Well ah… sure," I said, knowing I would be late for the meeting at Campbell Labs. But, Robert Campbell probably wouldn't even notice, the way he was organized.

We walked across the street to a hamburger stand and I had difficulty to take my eyes off her, observing how her hips flowed. She ordered two lemonades and I tried to pay, but she insisted, reaching into her shoulder bag and opening a purse. I saw her thumb through a stack of hundred-dollar bills until she came to a ten.

I carried the lemonades over to a wooden picnic table, where we took places under the shade of an umbrella.

We sat for a moment of silence and I wasn't sure what to say and then she asked, "Are you from around here?"

"Not really."

"Where are you from?" she asked.

Again, I noticed the creamy quality of her skin. "I grew up between West L.A. and Central L.A."

"That sounds like a tough area?"

"Kind of. You have to watch yourself. You ever been there?"

"No," she laughed. "Mainly Brentwood, Beverly Hills and Malibu whenever I come out here. You have to remember I come from the East Coast." She pressed her fingers to her chest and moved them across 'Vassar'. My eyes carefully followed.

"Does your family still live in Central L.A.?" she asked.

"Huh?"

She smiled. "Your family. Where do they live?"

"Oh. Don't really have any," I answered.

"You what?" she asked.

I always had difficulty to tell this. "I grew up in foster homes, all over Los Angeles County."

She paused and her eyes became sad. "How, ah, how did that work, or how was it?"

"A little bit out of your experience, huh?"

"Well, look, if you don't want to talk about it, it's okay. I didn't know when I asked about your family, that is, that you weren't, ah..."

"Not normal?"

Her neck blushed. "No, that's not what I meant. I didn't mean to take the conversation to an uncomfortable place."

I smiled. "No, don't worry about it. For some of us that's just how fate dealt its hand."

"So you don't have any parents or brothers or sisters?"

"I guess I could say that Clyde and Rochelle, my foster parents, are about the closest thing I've ever had to parents. They took me in when I was fifteen and have stuck with me since then. And as far as brothers and sisters, I've had dozens, if you want to look at it that way. There's one that's like a real brother. His name is Jake."

"Jake?" Her eyebrows went up.

"Yeah, Jake. He's a year younger than me and we've gone through a lot together. In fact, we could even pass as brothers. Same color of eyes, although he's blond. He's six foot five, about an inch taller than me, but I can still kick his butt."

She laughed. "Sounds like a brother."

"He's got a rough story, most recently going through a divorce from a wild woman called Martha. Now he's a short order cook at a place called Sloppy Sam's Hamburger Heaven over on Wiltshire Boulevard."

"That's too bad, about this Martha I mean."

"She's a mess," I said. "She'd do anything for money."

"Really? Who are this Clyde and Rochelle?"

"They are super good people and I was lucky to be placed with them. They sure made sure we got good grades. Clyde helped Jake and me get into UCLA. Who knows how we would have turned out" For some reason it seemed to me that our conversation was making her feel uncomfortable

She shifted forward. "So, what do you do in the evenings?" she asked.

"It probably sounds boring, but for the last year I've spent all my time working on a business idea I put together while doing my MBA. Most evenings are filled with that." She didn't need to know it was also an attempt to isolate myself from the world, having gone through some crappy relationships. Guys like me are fragile. Six foot four; two hundred and thirty five pounds of solid muscle, twenty-eight years old, and I still have the emotional maturity of a thirteen year old. Fragile.

"You live in an exciting city and you spend all your time working on a business thing. I can't believe it."

"I know," I said.

She moved her hand across the table, long fingers; perfectly manicured pink fingernails. "Do you ever eat?" she asked.

"Do I what?"

"Eat. Food. You know what that is?"

"Sure. Peanut butter sandwiches at least twice a week."

"No, what kind of food do you like? Mexican? Chinese? Italian? Hamburgers?"

"I'm not picky," I said. "What about you?"

"How about Mexican?" She asked. "Do you know of any good places?"

Was she asking me out? "Well, sure, I like Mexican food. How about you? Do you like real Mexican food?"

"What do you mean by 'real' Mexican?"

"It's the difference between artificial pueblo style chain restaurants versus genuine Mexican."

"There's this nice Mexican restaurant near Beverly Hills," she stated.

"How'd you like to try a place in Los Angeles? Nothing fancy, but the real thing."

An eyebrow lifted, eyes reflecting an apprehensive look. She said. "Sounds interesting. Tonight?"

"Tonight?" I was surprised.

"Sure, I'm headed to Brentwood now. I suggest we meet at a coffee shop just off of Rodeo Drive, as it's not all that far from where you live."

"How do you know that?" I asked.

Her eyes opened. "I, ah, I thought you weren't from around here, from, ah… your car, and you said you were from central L.A., so Rodeo Drive is what I mostly know in that direction and thought it would be a good place to meet. Is it close to where you live? We can meet somewhere else."

"No, that's okay. I actually live in Venice Beach, and you're right, it's not too far away."

"Venice Beach? After coming here for so many years I've never even been to the famous Venice Beach. I'd love to see it sometime," she said.

"It's a zoo," I said.

"My name's Janie Carlton," she said. "What's yours?"

"Hank. Hank Morgan."

And that's how it started, naturally, quickly, almost like she led me into it. At least that's how I interpreted it when I thought about it. She gave me the name of the coffee shop and said it was near some banks and lawyer's offices. Actually I had never been to Rodeo Drive, but meeting there would be perfect. It gave me time to visit Campbell Labs and then get home, shower, and put on some clean clothing. It also meant I didn't have to drive the twenty miles each way back and forth to Malibu. But for her I would have done it.

When we finished the lemonades, I got into my car and the doubts began to flood into my soul. A girl from Malibu carrying hundred dollar bills, who only knows Rodeo Drive, who is straight out of Vogue Magazine, or better yet Playboy, and she is asking me out to dinner?

This was all too good to be true, to have dinner with her. I chuckled; suspecting the place I was taking her was out of her normal routine.

But then my stomach churned. I wondered if this would only take me back into the pain pit?

CHAPTER 4

At seven o'clock I parked my jeep in front of the coffee shop just off of Rodeo Drive, quickly realizing my car was out of place compared to the shiny luxury cars that were everywhere. People walked by and stared at the large spot of gray antirust paint I had sprayed on one fender. It was a halfhearted effort to stop the rust from eating through. There was a finger-sized hole in the cloth top, like a mini sunroof.

Knowing where I was taking Janie, I wore jeans and a black open collared short-sleeved shirt like those worn by Hispanics. I didn't want to be too much out of place, because the neighborhood where we were going was unpredictable. At the same time, that's where you went to get real Mexican food, and I did know my way around that part of L.A.

The coffee shop was as she described it, surrounded by banks and lawyer's offices. I went inside and she was already there. She stood up when she saw me and smiled. My eyes almost popped out. She was wearing a lily-white crocheted camisole top showing off her perfect shoulders and full breasts. Tight citrus color cropped pants hugged her legs, accentuating her sleek figure. And on her feet were a pair of leather strapped sandals with tall stiletto heels. When she stood up she seemed only an inch or two shorter than me.

She wore turquoise earrings with a matching turquoise pendent necklace. The turquoise accentuated the color of her eyes. She had a pink and gray-striped jacket draped over her arm.

"Wow", I said. She was a knockout, like straight out of a fashion magazine.

People in the coffee shop stared at us, but maybe more at me than her, as I was the one who seemed out of place.

She had a smile on her face when she got into my Jeep, like getting into a ride at an amusement park. I caught the scent of an exquisite perfume that contrasted with the old engine smell of the car. I drove down to I-10 and went east and then south on Soto Street into the heart of East L.A. Eventually all the signs on the shops turned into Spanish. Colorful murals were on some walls and graffiti was on fences, mostly with Spanish words.

It was difficult to think that some miles from here was the color divide where the vast black section of L.A. began. I had spent time growing up on both sides of the divide, being with Hispanic foster parents until I was fifteen and then moving across.

Janie and I carried on small talk through the trip, but as we drove down Soto Street and crossed Ceasar Chavez I sensed she was becoming apprehensive.

"This is incredible," she stated.

"Why's that?" I asked.

"It's so colorful, so… disorganized. Is it safe here?"

"As much as anywhere, as long as you don't go looking for trouble." I knew that my car blended in and I was appropriately dressed. Now, Janie was another matter.

"You're sure? I've heard so much about gangs and shootings." She asked.

"Don't worry. We're okay. I think you'll like where we're going."

I found a place to park and we walked half a block until we came to a solid wooden faced building painted in baby blue. It had no windows. 'Mama Caterina's Restaurante' was painted in red on the side in Hispanic style lettering. The place used to be an unused rundown storage building until Mama Caterina took it over. The buildings on either side were covered with graffiti, but not Mama Caterina's.

We went through the front door, entered a noisy room, and were greeted by a teenage girl wearing traditional Mexican dress.

"*Buenas tardes*," she said. Her dark eyes drifted to Janie and she scanned her up and down.

"I called and made reservations for two."

She looked at me inquisitively.

I said, "Hank Morgan. Tengo *reservaciones para dos personas*. "

"*Ah, si, Senor Morgan.*" She smiled. "*Bien Venido*".

She led the way and we walked through a crowded room full of families with children where the Spanish language filled the air. The noise level dropped as we passed by them, a six foot four inch Anglo with a very much out of place blond haired beauty queen. We entered a large courtyard where irregular ceramic tiles covered the floor. Janie grabbed my arm for support, having some difficulty with her stiletto-heeled sandals.

We were led to a small round wooden table and sat on wicker chairs covered with cushions. Grape vines hung on trellises above our heads and in the corner of the courtyard two musicians sat on wooden chairs on a small stage and played guitars and sang songs in Spanish. It was quieter here than in the interior room, as people lowered their conversations in order to listen to the musicians.

A woman dressed in traditional Mexican dress with long thick gray hair walked through the courtyard. It was Mama Caterina. She smiled as she approached our table, stretched out her hands, grabbed me behind the neck and gave me a motherly kiss on the cheek.

"Hank, Hank," she said. "It is too long. Each time I see you, you are more handsome, from little boy to big handsome hombre."

It had been five or six months since I had last been here, back when I still had a little spare cash.

Mama Caterina turned and looked at Janie. "Hank, *esta senorita es muy bonita. Tienes mucho suerte.*"

Janie had a quizzical look on her face.

"She said you are very beautiful." I said.

Janie smiled and said, "Thank you."

"And that he is lucky," Mama Caterina added. "He is a good boy and we have to feed him well."

There was no need to order. The waiter brought grilled chicken with green and red peppers, fresh tortillas, enchiladas, enough food to feed an army. Mama Caterina brought two bottles of cold Mexican beer and put them on the table and then left.

I grinned at Janie. "Are you legal?"

"Legally twenty-six," Janie laughed. "How do you know her, Mama Caterina?"

"I used to live around here and even worked for her for a few summers, washing dishes, until I was fifteen. Then I moved to another foster home. But I try and get back here every few months, to touch base with my roots."

"Your roots?"

"As much as you can have them," I stated.

"Then why did you move away?"

"Something happened. There was some trouble."

"Trouble."

"I got into a fight. You know, kid's stuff. And the Social Services thought it was better that I moved to another place." Janie didn't need to know the details.

"Where did you go?"

"Just a few miles from here, with Clyde and Rochelle." In reality it was like moving to another planet.

"And somehow you eventually ended up graduating from UCLA and are starting a company."

"Trying to."

"I'd like to hear about it," she said, bending forward. The top of her low cut camisole slightly dropped revealing her round smooth breasts.

"Like what?" I asked, distracted from her question.

She reached across and ran a finger across my hand. "Well, you know. How did you get the idea? Where do you stand with your project? I wouldn't think of a lifeguard, of someone who grew up in a neighborhood like this, as going into some kind of technology thing. You just sound so interesting."

"I ah… well." I wasn't sure I had told her anything about my project or the technology component, but maybe I had, and I wasn't really clear about what I had said, because her fingers on my hand sent shivers up my spine. I took a sip of beer and told her the history.

CHAPTER 5

I didn't tell her the part about knocking out a drill sergeant in the Marines, but that was how my idea started, or at least it put me into the place where I got my idea. The sergeant was demonstrating self-defense to the recruits and was roughing us up to show that he was boss. Because of my size or whatever, he somehow took a dislike to me and when he got me into the training pit he started getting overly physical, slapping me on the face, challenging me to attack him, ridiculing me in front of the others. His idea was for me to attack and then he would use one of his techniques to subdue me.

In spite of his commands I didn't attack, but just stood there and took his slaps without moving and that made him angry, and he started to call me a coward and all kinds of other names to get me to attack him. When that didn't work he hit me in the stomach and it took the wind out of me, but I straightened back up to take some more.

Then he called me "chicken-shit" and started to swing at me again, but his defenses were down, so I unloaded a kick into his groin and when he bent over with his hands on his testicles I kneed him in the chin. He landed on his back and I dove on top of him and began to pound his face with my fist.

The recruits just stood there and watched for a while until some other sergeants started to yell and then the recruits swarmed onto me and tried to pull me off. I knocked out one and bloodied the noses of several others. The sergeant just lay there on the ground and didn't move and the next thing I knew, I was in the brig. In some way it was a replay of what happened when I was fifteen.

I was in the brig for a few hours, but I got lucky. It seemed the drill sergeant had overstepped Marine regulations and the Master Sergeant didn't want to let this get out of hand, so he asked that we all just forgive and forget. I think the Master Sergeant saw some humor in this. The drill sergeant ended up with some pretty mean looking black eyes and from that point on they kept me away from him. My choice was either to leave the Marines or accept special duty. I took the special duty not wanting to look like a failure in front of Clyde and Rochelle.

So, for two years I had my routine. For half the day I did special duty working with the self-defense instructors. They made me do the dirty work. The Master Sergeant didn't want any of his drill sergeants crossing any lines, so they used me instead. They gave me the title of self-defense instructor. I had my share of fights growing up, but that experience taught me a lot more in that I encountered just about every attacking technique possible and most Marine recruits are already pretty tough guys. It also helped me deal with this aggression problem I have. But it's still not solved. I didn't tell this to Janie.

The other half day I had a different job.

That part I told her about. I said, "Basically they assigned me to the commissary where we had truckloads of supplies coming and going each day. It was there that I worked out some methods of controlling the flow of materials; formulating some ideas, testing them, and making the place run more efficiently. I probably saved American taxpayers millions of dollars in terms of goods not being lost, not that anyone really cared. But, I got this idea that my methods might work outside of the Marines, like for companies."

"But, how did you get from there to here?" She asked.

"Well, when I left the Marines I kept thinking about the idea and discussed it with Clyde, and he helped me get into UCLA. There I majored in business and took lots of courses in Operations Management, besides all the normal stuff they require. The idea just kept growing in my mind and I began to work out models, both on paper and computer based. After I completed my Bachelor's degree, Clyde advised that I needed more training, so I went into the UCLA MBA program, focusing on entrepreneurship. And, I continued to develop the idea."

"So is that when you started your company?" she asked, gently pressing her fingers against my forearm.

"Yeah. After I graduated with the MBA I got job offers from some large companies, but Clyde encouraged me to pursue my idea. He even loaned me a thousand dollars, which I combined with what I had managed to save from my lifeguard jobs, and I started to develop the idea on my own, working in the garage below my apartment. Then I met with Robert Campbell who runs Campbell Labs over in Culver City and took him in as a business partner."

"You have a partner?" She seemed surprised.

"I needed help and he now owns twenty percent of TechZip and I own the rest. Robert is a guy with a lot of experience, a scientist, I guess in his mid fifties. He's got about twenty or thirty very strange software and hardware engineers working there with him, a bunch of guys who get excited about the most obscure technical things you can imagine. The tag line on the company stationary is, 'Campbell Labs: The Super-Geeks who make things work when you can't'."

Janie laughed. "You're kidding?"

"No. That's the truth. They do prototyping for companies. It's an extremely unorganized place, but a lot of different technology companies come to Robert when they need help in developing new products. When I shared my idea with Robert, he got excited and started to develop some working models, which first ended up as software code. Then he developed a kind of barcode reader that can pick up a wireless signal, so that anyone can have a mobile device for inventory monitoring."

"Why is that so important?" She asked.

"It's like a virtual inventory monitoring system that does continual cycle counting, only automatic without having to physically pick up each item. I had some ideas and Robert worked out the technology, even adding functionality here and there that I didn't think about. Through the software it can interface into most standard inventory control packages used by large corporations."

"That's amazing," she stated.

"It's like a very advanced and cost effective method of inventory control, and can work in just about any situation. Robert also helped submit the patent application."

"You've got a patent?" She asked.

"Just an application, but we're pretty sure a patent will be granted. This is very advanced stuff."

"That's so interesting," she commented.

"Really?" I asked. I could see how it would be interesting to someone running a stockroom or trying to improve the efficiency of their supplies operations, but interesting to a hot-chick from Malibu?

"No, it is," she said. "You wouldn't think that someone with your, ah… history would make it so far in doing something so fantastic." She looked in my eyes and ran her fingers up my arm. "And you said you started from a garage. I think that many of the people who started companies in Silicon Valley started in garages. You're just like one of them."

"Fat chance," I said. "I ran out of cash and don't have any idea when this thing will get off the ground."

"Well, it will," She said. "You just need to have patience. I'd love to see your garage, to see this place that will be a historical monument some day. You know like the garage of Bill Packard and Dave Hewlett in San Francisco; that's a historical monument."

It was the other way around, Bill Hewlett and Dave Packard, and it's in Palo Alto, but I let it go. There was no way I could take her to my place. It was way below her league, and anyway, what was I doing with a girl like this who dresses in Gucci and Pierre Cardin and carries hundred dollar bills in her purse?

"Ah… my garage isn't that important. How did you like the meal?"

"It was wonderful."

The musicians were playing a slow melodic Mexican song, *"Los canciones de mi padre"*, something that my Latino foster parents used to sing. It brought back nostalgic memories. I never knew my real father. He got my mother pregnant and then he went back to Louisiana, at least that's what I remembered someone saying, and what's on the records at the Social Services. The records said his occupation was Longshoreman and I wondered if that's what he was still doing.

I paid for the meal and we said goodbye to Mama Caterina. She kissed me on both cheeks and then she kissed Janie and she told Janie to be careful with me and we walked outside to the sidewalk and toward the car.

I had to walk slowly because of Janie's stiletto heels, but I was surprised how she could navigate on them. She took my arm and leaned into me and I felt the softness of her breast against me. It's moments like that where words are hard to come, so we continued walking and I wasn't really paying attention until we came right up to two guys leaning against a car. From the color of their bandanas I knew right away we might be in trouble. We had a saga from the past.

One of them stepped directly in front of me, the other a little off to his left. "Hey gringo," the closest one said. "Can you loan me some money?"

They were both around six feet tall. The one in front of me was wiry and the one behind him was large and meaty, his tick arms covered with tattoos.

"*No quiero problemas*," I said.

The first one smiled. "We don't want trouble either. Only *dinero*. Give us some and you may go."

Janie slowly moved around behind me.

"There is no money for you," I said. "Now, we go on our way."

"You do not listen well," the first one said. "This is our street and we charge you money to use it. Now you give me your wallet and the sack." He nodded down to Janie's handbag which I assumed still had the hundred dollar bills.

I hadn't noticed, but his hand was down and he lifted it, pushed a button, and quickly a long sharp knife blade appeared.

In that situation it's better to move fast to catch them off guard, so without hesitating I reached out and grabbed his hand and with a forceful twist I moved his hand downward and inward, putting my weight into it until I felt his wrist crack. The shinny knife clinked onto the pavement. He bent forward in pain while grabbing his broken wrist with his free hand, and at that moment I kicked high into his ribs and there was a loud crack and he groaned out, "Ahhhhh…," and he fell on his knees on the ground. I quickly kicked him again and he rolled into a fetal position.

The second one was now in action. He was reaching around behind his back and I knew it could only mean a handgun so in one quick thrust with the bottom of my right hand I unloaded a powerful blow to his nose and I felt cartilage break. His hands were coming up and before they got to his face I hooked with my left hand into his jaw and he went down like a felled log hitting the ground.

They both lay there, one groaning, the other out cold and my instinct was to stomp their heads into bloody mash, and while lifting my foot to do so I glanced and saw Janie standing there with her eyes wide open, and I immediately stopped and reached out to hold her up. Then behind her I saw two guys running in our direction. I turned and just in front of me was a guy with the same color bandana as the two on the ground.

He had a gun pointed at my head.

CHAPTER 6

"**K**eel him Jacko," the guy on the ground moaned. The guy with the gun looked at me and smiled. "What have you done to my *amigos*?" He asked.

"They got in my way," I said, now knowing who he was. Jacko. He had a reputation.

"You show no respect for my neighborhood," Jacko said.

"You show no respect for visitors," I replied.

"You talk arrogant."

The gun was pointed at my head. He stood about three steps in front of me. Had he been just a bit closer I would have gone for him, but with Janie there I didn't want a stray bullet going off in the wrong direction.

"Mama Caterina would not like to know that her clients were treated badly."

"Mama Caterina?" Jacko glanced in the direction of the restaurant and he smiled. "You hide behind the skirts of a woman?"

"Never, but you know what she'll do if she hears about this.

The guy on the ground whimpered. "Shoot him and take his money." He was having trouble sitting up. The other one was still out cold, blood flowing from his nose.

Jacko looked at me and then at Janie. "Money is not important. I'll just take *la chica* instead." His eyes scanned Janie from top to bottom.

"Don't even think about it. Otherwise you end up like Romero Rodriguez," I said.

Jacko tilted his head to the side and looked at me through squinted eyes. "Hey, I know you. The crazy *gringo*." He stepped back a couple of steps and looked at me and smiled. "You are bigger now, and it was maybe ten years ago or so, but *los Chicanos* still talk about you. What is your name?"

"Morgan."

"Yes, Morgan it is. You did a good thing. Romero was *un hombre muy malo*, but he still has some friends here." He took another step back, slightly bowed and waved his the gun in a downward movement. "You may use this street whenever you want. Morgan, *amigo*."

"*Gracias*," I said.

I held Janie by the arm and we headed for my car.

"Jacko, Shoot him now," the guy on the ground said.

I turned and saw Jacko push his foot into the guy's ribs. "*Callate carbon. Es Morgan. No Sabes?*"

The guy on the ground grunted.

Just before getting to my car Jacko cried out. "Hey Morgan, *amigo.*"

"*Que pasa?*" I asked.

"When you get tired of *la chica*, I will take her. Just let me know." He laughed.

I smiled and said, "I will let you know."

Janie's eyes became round. We got into the car and headed back towards Rodeo Drive.

I regretted the incident, a nice dinner gone bad.

★ ★ ★

For the first five miles Janie didn't say a word, her eyes fixed directly on the freeway in front of her. Then she took a deep breath and asked, "Who was Romero Rodriguez?"

"I don't know what he was talking about." I didn't want to go into that.

"But, he knew your name," she said.

"You know, things get confused in these neighborhoods. Rumors start and then they get blown out of proportion."

"But, he had a gun pointed at your head and you seemed to take it so calmly."

"Where I grew up it is part of life." In actuality my nerves were jumping back there, but it is true that street kids react differently to these sorts of things.

"And you speak Spanish," she stated.

"Enough. Well, to be honest I'm fluent and speak like one of them. Same dialect. That's why we, ah… bonded."

"Bonded? You took out two guys like it was nothing, like swatting flies. One was still knocked out when we drove away and might even be dead, and you treat it so casually." The palm of her hand was pointed at me, slightly shaking.

"He was breathing. He'll be alright after the nose heals."

"That's what I mean. You're so casual about it."

I didn't really think about it, being casual. Sure, my adrenaline was flowing, but had she not been there I would have smashed their heads into the sidewalk. Rochelle spent hours with me on this, but the feelings are still there that make me do it.

Things got quiet again and I drove on to Rodeo Drive. Janie just kept staring out the window, like deep in thought and I was wondering what she was thinking.

"Where shall I take you?" I asked.

I shook her concentration and her head jerked up. "Oh, just back to the coffee shop. I'll head back to Malibu from there."

"Shall I take you to your car?"

"No, it's okay."

I parked the jeep near the coffee shop, turned off the engine and then looked at Janie.

"Look, I'm sorry it turned out like this. I wanted it to be an exceptional time, going to a restaurant that was maybe a bit different."

"I've never experienced anything like this." Janie said. "The food and atmosphere at Mama Caterina's was amazing and this other thing that happened out on the street was unbelievable, like out of a movie, only it wasn't. You were exceptional... and to think you are starting a company." She took a long pause. "In Venice Beach. It's so interesting."

I didn't know where she was going, but I felt relieved that this wasn't a totally negative experience. "Then, I'm ah... wondering if, ah..."

"I'd love to go out with you again Hank. This is a whole new world. What are you doing tomorrow night?"

"Nothing. Tomorrow's a day off and the evening is free." I had planned to spend it working in my garage and at Campbell Labs.

"Let's do something then," she said. "Can you come to the place in Malibu for lunch and then I'll leave the evening up to you."

"The place? You mean your house in Malibu."

"My house? Yes, that's what I meant, our place."

"In the evening do you want to stay on your side of the tracks and play it safe?" I smiled.

"Definitely not. Take me somewhere. Show me things. I'd like to see your garage."

From her purse she took a small notebook and scribbled something on it, tore off the page and handed it to me. "That's my address and cell phone number. Can you be there at twelve thirty for lunch?"

"Sure, that's great," I said, adjusting tomorrow's schedule in my mind.

I got out of the Jeep and walked around to the other side of the car and opened the door for her. She got out and stood in front of me and then she moved toward me and pressed her body into mine and I felt her form and it pleased me. And then she brought her lips to mine and kissed me. It happened so fast and unexpectedly that I didn't have time to really respond.

She pulled away and said, "I'll see you tomorrow at my place."

And then she turned and walked in the direction of the coffee shop.

★ ★ ★

I got back into the Jeep and started it, my nerves shaking, realizing her body and kiss touched me deeply, rattling me more than the experience with Jacko and his gang members. But, I wondered why she didn't want me to take her to her car, so I drove around the block and turned into a small alley and parked the Jeep and quickly ran back to some bushes where I could see the coffee shop.

She was there standing by the glass door like she was waiting, and then she opened the door and walked in the opposite direction from me. She went half a block and then disappeared into an underground parking that was below a five-story marble and glass office building.

I waited, and a few minutes later saw a red Ferrari come out of the parking lot and she was driving it. And I couldn't believe it. What was she doing driving a Ferrari, and even more so, what was she doing with a guy like me, riding around in a beat up fifteen year old Jeep?

Logically she should have turned right to head in the direction of I-10 as the fastest way back to Malibu, but she turned left in the direction of Brentwood and got caught behind a red light.

I sprinted back to my Jeep, started it and pulled out into the side street where she couldn't directly see me. I was curious to know where she was headed. The traffic light turned green and I waited and after she was a couple of blocks down the street I drove out. The light had turned red again, but I saw no cars coming, so I just went through it.

She was well ahead of me and I managed to keep her in sight. She finally went into Beverly Hills where there were larger houses with more trees and shrubs and she drove to a gated house.

As she arrived a large metal gate opened and she drove through. I didn't continue up the street, but made a note of the address and headed back towards my place in Venice Beach wondering who she was and what was going on; a classy chick who shops at Rodeo Drive, has hundred dollar bills in her purse, drives a Ferrari and enters a gated house in Beverly Hills?

But mostly I thought about her body pressed against mine, and the low cut camisole top.

CHAPTER 7

That night I didn't sleep well tossing and turning, wishing the incident had not happened outside the restaurant. Everything was perfect up until then. The other thing was, she turned me on in a bad way. But at the bottom of it was what a girl like that would be doing with a guy like me?

In the morning I got up, showered and dressed, and drove over to Sloppy Sam's Hamburger Heaven. It's in an old building that's squeezed between glass tower office buildings. The building has been owned for fifty years by Samouel Thanos who originated from Greece. Now he's just known as 'Sam'.

For years property speculators have been trying to buy him out, but he has refused. He's now in his seventies and continues to run it. It's a popular breakfast and lunch place for people in the business district.

As I walked in Elena, a young Ukranian who works as a waitress there greeted me. Big smile. "Heennk. *Priviette.* Good specials today. Goulash or Moussaka." She's a blond, blue-eyed girl in her early twenties who came to the U.S. a couple of years ago.

"*Posiba* Elena. Is Jake here?" She recently taught me how to say thank you in Ukranian.

"Jake is in the back," she said, nodding her head toward the kitchen. She carried a pot of black coffee in her right hand, poured some into a cup and handed it to me.

I took a sip and then made my way toward the kitchen where the other waiters, bus boys, and cooks were standing around Sam. Jake was there. They were mainly a mix of eastern European nationalities. Sam once told me that he only hired Orthodox Christians and nothing else, as they were the only ones who knew how to work like he wanted to work. Why he hired Jake I will never know

When Sam saw me he looked up and said, "Hank. What you like better, goulash or moussaka?"

"Moussaka," I said.

Sam turned to his crew. "Moussaka it is. That's the lunch special. Now go."

"But I can't stay for lunch," I said.

"Doesn't matter. We do it for you." He laughed. "You come back another time and I make you Moussaka."

"Thanks Samouel," I said as I made my way over to Jake who was pouring some pancake batter on the griddle.

"Hey man. How's the lifeguard?" Jake asked.

"Okay. How's the cook?" This is what he dropped out of a UCLA MBA to do, just a couple of classes shy of graduating. Now he's a six foot five inch, blond haired, blue eyed, overly educated short order cook. He does have kind of a Russian look. Maybe that's why Sam hired him. In reality Jake was an abandoned kid and the Social Services had no record of his parents or origins.

"The cook's good. I like it here," Jake said. "This is like family."

"I know. They're good people aren't they."

"Yeah." He flipped the pancakes, let them cook a bit and then put them onto a plate. He put a liberal portion of butter and maple syrup on the pancakes and handed the plate to me. "Forks are in the normal place." He pointed.

"Thanks." I found a fork in a tray full of eating utensils, cut into the pancakes and took a bite. "That's good," I said. Outside of Mama Caterina's meal last night and the pancakes this morning, it seemed like I'd existed on cornflakes and noodles for the past weeks. "Can I ask your advice?" I asked.

"Sure, you've got that 'I need pancakes and advice' kind of look on your face. What's up?"

"Girl questions."

"Oh, here we go again." Jake's eyes rolled up as he put a mound of raw hamburger into a frying pan.

"Yeah, maybe."

"So, what's going on."

I told him about meeting Janie yesterday, how we went to Mama Caterina's and the rumble with Jacko's gang. Then I told him about the Ferrari and following her to Beverly Hills.

Jake whistled. "No kidding. A Ferrari."

'Yeah and she's built like Miss Universe, only more so. How do you read this?"

"Rich girl is turned on by bad boy kind of thing," he stated.

"What do you mean?"

"Look. If she's got all the money you say she has and a Ferrari, maybe she's just getting tired of all the toys and the snobby rich boys. You're something new, giving her some fun she never had before, like a new level of experience."

"You're saying like a new toy?"

"Boy toy. Yeah, something like that."

"So, I'm a new toy. What does that mean?"

"It means enjoy it, but don't get carried away with her. When she gets tired of you she'll just jump to the next thing. There's nothing solid there. But if she's got money, then maybe she'll throw some funding into TechZip. Opportunity is hard to come by, so see if you can hit on her for that."

Jake was slightly younger than me, but his failed marriage with 'Hell on Wheels' Martha gave him some unique insights when it came to women.

"So where do I take it from here?"

"What are you doing tonight?" he asked.

"I don't know"

"I'm taking Elena the waitress to a concert tonight, kind of a strange combination of rap and historical Motown. Brother's Club. Want to come?"

I thought about it. What happened with Jacko last night was an exception. Jake and I had gone to concerts before and while they tended to be loud and rambunctious, it was usually a fun affair. Sometimes though it could get rough. "Okay, that sounds outside her league. Tell me when and where to meet you."

"Eight o'clock at Clyde and Rochelle's place. We can go together from there." Jake looked up from the frying pan and turned toward me. "Be careful man."

"Thanks."

* * *

I left Sloppy Sam's Hamburger Heaven and drove to Culver City into an industrial zone and parked in front of a building that looked like an old airplane hanger. I walked past the reception desk that never had anybody there and entered a large cavernous room full of tables covered with computers in various states of assembly, test and measurement equipment, wires, an enormous variety of chips, circuit boards, and soldering stuff. The room was full of geeky guys who were bent over tables working on things or staring at computer screens.

Robert Campbell was standing at a table looking at a large piece of paper that seemed to be a circuit design. He looked up at me. "Wrong wiring. See this? That connection should be going over here." There were literally thousands of red, blue and green lines that filled the paper all intertwined and connected to each other in some way. He pointed at a small obscure red line that went from one square box to another. "Makes all the difference. Won't work unless you get it right. Unipac has been struggling for months with this thing and now they brought it to me."

I knew about Unipac, one of the largest electronic companies in Silicon Valley, with manufacturing divisions in L.A. They were one of the clients of Campbell Labs.

Before I could say anything Robert said, "Come here.' He waved his hand for me to follow him.

We came to a table that had a Tablet on it with a small device inserted into the USB slot. "The wireless device?" I asked.

"Works like a dream. Picks up all the signals. Now you have a pretty powerful package with the inventory control software. With one push of the button it could remotely read everything in this room and tell me what is out of place or missing."

I looked around the room at the mounds of equipment and random things everywhere. "Out of place? You mean you've counted everything in here?"

Robert laughed. "Of course not. I'm speaking hypothetically."

"But, you're saying it works."

"That's what I'm saying. It works a thousand times better than anything else that's out there, maybe even a million times better."

"I can't believe it," I said. This was too good to be true. Six years of thinking about this, constantly working on it in my mind, and one year of fully dedicated work and now there is a product that works.

"Proof of principle," Robert said. "That's the first step in building your company, to prove that you have a product or service that works. But, now comes the hard part."

I couldn't think of what would be harder than what I had already done. "The hard part?"

Robert laughed. "You gotta find customers who will buy it, and you've got to make it and deliver it to them."

"You're right," I said, knowing I had a whole section on this in my written business plan. But the theoretical reality of the plan sort of hits you when you are facing the real world. Now I had a real live product. "Where do you think I should take it from here."

"To let people know about it," Robert said. "But don't worry. I already started some of that. My communications guy sent press releases to some trade journals." He nodded in the direction of Freddy, hunkered down in front of a computer screen, a skinny little guy who looked about seventeen years old. "Let's let the bait sit out there for a few days to see if we get any nibbles. Then we'll see how to take it from there."

About a month ago my company and product was highlighted in a small article in a technical magazine and my name was mentioned, but now it looked like we had a real product to talk about.

This was all good news that things were progressing and it gave me motivation to keep the project on track.

⋆ ⋆ ⋆

I drove north on Pacific Coast Highway toward Malibu thinking about the good news from Robert Campbell. Maybe things weren't as bad as I had thought. I now had a product that worked and Robert felt it could outperform anything on the market. We needed to move fast. In fact, I was glad there were only two weeks left with the lifeguard job, although every dollar earned through it would be of help. Two more weeks would add more to the cash reserve and I was grateful for that.

This was an entirely new ballgame for me. While I had the initial idea for the product, what did I really know about marketing other than some courses at UCLA? Textbooks were one thing, but I had never really done it in real life. That made me nervous. What happened if some large company learned about my idea and then threw some of their in house research and development guys on it and came up with a superior product? That was the war being played in the technology world. Whatever happened, we needed to move fast on this.

As I drove along, I looked at the address that Janie gave me. It was at Paradise Cove. I knew about it but had never been to that area before. It was known as being a place where movie stars and rich people lived. That made me nervous. In fact, everything about Janie made me nervous, her clothes, her car, her looks, and how she came on to me. Jake said it was the rich girl, bad boy thing, yet I didn't really look at myself as the bad boy. At least I was trying to change my ways from the past.

Yet, the incident from last night reinforced that. Maybe that's what she saw in me and in fact Jake was right. I was just a new exotic boy toy that she would use and then throw away. Yet, she seemed to take a genuine interest in me and in what I was doing.

I decided to play it through, to have lunch with her today and take her out tonight and then see where it would go from there. Jake said to be careful and that was good advice, yet when I was around her my heart just seemed to melt.

I drove down Paradise Cove Road for about half a mile and I saw the number she had given me, and drove through an open metal gate into a small access road. There was a large parking area and on one side was a garage. I counted four doublewide car doors. The Ferrari wasn't in the parking area.

I got out and rang the doorbell and waited. A few minutes later a maid came to the door, at least I could tell with how she was dressed. She was Hispanic and looked to be in her thirties.

"Hello, I'm Hank Morgan, here to see Janie, ah…Carlton."

"Come," the maid said, without smiling.

I felt like speaking Spanish with her, but didn't want to embarrass her.

She led me into a large living room with huge glass windows that looked out on the ocean. The room had a long couch that looked to be covered in white silk, comfortable looking armchairs in green, and a large teak coffee table. Original paintings of Picasso, Miro and Roy Liechtenstein hung on the large white walls. At least when I got up close I could see that they weren't prints like my cheapo reproduction of Millet.

Janie came out from a side hallway. She was wearing a gray t-shirt tied in a knot at her belly and very short shorts. She was barefooted.

"Hello Hank. I'm so glad you came." She came over to me, went up on her tiptoes and gave me a hug and then a kiss on the cheek. I wasn't sure she was wearing anything under the t-shirt. She said, "Lola. We'll eat down at the pool house. Come on Hank, let me show you around."

We spent twenty minutes going through the estate where she showed me the main house with the five bedrooms, and the Spanish style pool house next to the swimming pool on the lower level. Beyond that was a tennis court. She pointed out the guesthouse down by the beach but didn't take me down to see it, explaining that is where she stayed most of the time when she came out to L.A.

I noticed a wire fence that ran around the property along with some surveillance cameras.

We finally settled at a table in the shade at the Spanish style pool house where there was a large tossed green salad and a plate of cold chicken cuts that were set out. A bottle of California Chardonnay was in a wine cooler next to the table.

Janie served two plates of salad and chicken and asked me to pour the wine. Then she raised her glass and said, "Sante".

I raised mine. "Salud".

"This place is very nice," I said meaning that the place was outstanding. "You come here every summer?"

"Not quite," she said.

"How long has your father had it?"

"Some years, but it is not my father's. It's like an uncle."

"Well, it sure is beautiful." I tasted the wine. It was the best I had ever had, not that I was an expert in wine. I looked around and thought of the contrast of where I lived and knew I'd be too embarrassed to take her to my place.

We carried on with small talk and she didn't mention the incident with Jacko's gang the night before. When lunch was finished she called Lola the maid who came and took away the dishes.

"Do you want to swim?" She asked.

"Didn't you hear about swimming too soon after lunch? It's dangerous." I laughed.

"Don't worry. I've got a lifeguard."

"I don't have a swimsuit," I said.

"We don't use them around here." She had a small grin on her face.

"You're kidding."

"No, but if you are so prudish, you can get one in the back room there." She pointed into the pool house.

I glanced up and saw that one of the surveillance cameras had shifted position. It was no longer pointed outside the property, but was directly facing toward us. It gave me an uneasy feeling.

I went into the back of the pool house and saw a pile of men's swimsuits, all new in their original packaging. I took one my size and quickly changed.

When I went back to the pool, Janie was already in it and I was a bit disappointed to see that she was wearing a pink bikini, but it was mighty small. I dove in and she followed after me and we splashed each other for a while and then ended up in the Jacuzzi where her leg touched mine and I was tempted to push it further, but saw that the surveillance camera had shifted position again and was pointed at us. Someone was watching us and I didn't know why or who.

Finally Janie said, "So, what's the plan for this evening?"

I felt like testing her and said, "Do you like adventure?"

"Anything like last night?" She asked.

"Last night was kid's stuff compared to where we can go. Are you game?"

"You won't tell me?" she asked.

"No."

"Okay, I'm game. Is it in L.A.?"

"I can at least tell you that. Sure."

"Then why don't we go into L.A. now, maybe do some shopping or you can show me Venice Beach. I'll drive my car in so you don't have to come back here tonight to bring me home."

"That's fine, but why don't we just meet up at the coffee shop at Rodeo Drive?" I didn't want her anywhere near my place in Venice Beach. It was way below her class, but I didn't want to make it too obvious that I was embarrassed to take her there.

Her eyes dropped and I saw her quickly glancing at the surveillance camera. Then she perked up. "What should I wear tonight?"

"What you had last night was a knockout," I said.

"I can't wear the same thing two nights in a row!"

"You could wear it every day between here and eternity and I'd be thrilled."

"We'll see," she said.

We walked up to the main house and then out to my car. On a key chain she pushed a button and a garage door opened and there I saw the red Ferrari.

"That's your car?" I asked, trying to sound surprised.

"A gift from my family, my uncle."

"Not bad. Makes my car look just a tiny bit under classed."

"Your car is fun," she said. "What time do you want to meet at the coffee shop?"

"Seven thirty. We have to meet some people at eight."

"Sounds intriguing. See you there."

I got into my Jeep and drove down the entrance road and saw that a surveillance camera was following the movement of my car. I don't know why, but somehow I had the feeling that the equation had a different complexity, much more than what Jake said about it being a rich girl turned on by bad boy kind of thing.

CHAPTER 8

W e met at seven thirty at the coffee shop and she offered to take the Ferrari, but I knew it would probably be stolen in three minutes where we going, so we took the Jeep. She was dressed similar to last night, except all the colors were different. Her power pink camisole top seemed even lower than before and I wondered at what point she would get arrested for indecent exposure.

I was wearing mostly dark, with the same dark jeans as the night before, and a jet-black t-shirt. Again, I wanted to blend in, but tonight we would definitely stand out, especially when I saw how Janie was dressed.

We drove to South Central L.A. and I turned onto a residential street of rectangular wooden houses. They were all built in the fifties and hadn't had much renovation since then. On this street there was an attempt to keep yards clean and geraniums and other flowers were growing in some of them. Clyde ran a neighborhood-pride organization and people did their best to maintain things as well as they could, but they didn't have much money.

In reality, Clyde and Rochelle could have moved out of this neighborhood, as they both had decent jobs, but their sense of social responsibility kept them here. Rochelle said it was here that they had their best "ministry."

I parked behind Jake's car and turned off the engine.

"Where are we?" Janie asked. Her eyes shifted up and down the street.

"Clyde and Rochelle's. My last foster parents, over there." I pointed to a faded yellow house across the street.

"That's where you lived?" She asked.

"Yeah, for almost four years."

"But, isn't this a black section of town?"

"I guess," I said. "But, who cares. They are like my mother and father."

"They're black?"

"Well, you just said this is a black section of town."

"I can't believe it," she said. "You grew up with Mexicans and blacks."

"I grew up wherever social services sent me, and I lucked out when I landed with Clyde and Rochelle. They have been really good to me.

Come on.”

I went around to her side of the car and opened the door and she got out. We went across the street and I knocked on the front door and opened it before anyone could answer. Janie followed me.

Immediately familiar things hit my senses, the smell of Rochelle's famous chocolate chip cookies cooking in the oven, and laughter coming from different parts of the house.

In the living room there were three long couches of different colors and shapes, and an indeterminate number of folding chairs stacked against one wall. Sometimes ten or more people came here for Sunday lunches. Reproductions of paintings were on the walls; Renoir, Rembrandt, and a small wooden cross hanging slightly ajar above the door to the hall.

Clyde was seated on one of the couches and he rose when I entered the room. Jake and Elena were sitting on another couch. A black girl, well I guess you would say 'young woman', was sitting on the other couch. She was attractive and somehow she looked familiar.

Clyde exuberated, "Hank. How's it going?" He stood up, came over to me, arms open wide, and gave me one of his crushing bear hugs. He was as broad as I was. "Come on in man. Who's this fine looking lady?" He stood back and looked at her like checking out a new car.

"This is Janie. Janie, Clyde," I said.

He stuck out his big mitt of a hand and wrapped it around Janie's and shook it. "Well, have a seat." He pointed to the couch where he had been sitting.

Janie and I moved to the couch and Jake looked at me and quickly rolled his eyes, like one of those *oh boy are you ever in trouble* kind of looks.

We sat down and I introduced Janie to Jake and Elena. Elena wore a white blouse with a gold cross on a chain hanging down on the front, one of Samouel Thanos' Orthodox workers.

Clyde took a place on the couch next to the girl and said, "Hank, you remember Sharlee."

"Ah…," I looked again at the girl next to him and remembered. She attended the same Baptist church where Clyde and Rochelle took us each Sunday. I remembered her as this cute skinny young teenager about five or six years younger than me. She had this huge crush on me, always laughing and always following me around. "Sharlee. I'm sorry. I hardly recognized you. How are you doing?" The happy skinny duckling had become a swan. I was blown over.

"Fine. I haven't seen you for a few years Hank."

Clyde interjected. "Sharlee just graduated from Cal State Fullerton, Social Work, and is here to talk about any job opportunities in the Social Services."

"I guess you're the expert. What are the possibilities?" I asked.

Clyde lifted his shoulders. "Well, we have to stay positive, but there have been some cutbacks and you know how the seniority system works. Not much room for newcomers. But we gotta keep faith."

I nodded, knowing how much emphasis Clyde and Rochelle always put on faith, faith in God, faith in the system, faith that people can change. Jake and I were part of that faith, although he and I didn't have much of it.

As I looked at Sharlee my memories came back. She had an older sister, Martine, maybe my age, the best looking girl in church. I wanted to take her out, but there was this unspoken color divide, and Clyde and Rochelle were pretty straight about us being alone with girls. And, I don't think Mrs. Jackson, their mother, would have accepted it, as she was highly protective of her daughters. She was raising them on her own and did her best to keep them out of trouble, which I'm sure I represented. They never missed a Sunday at church, always dressed in simple clean pressed cotton dresses.

I turned to Sharlee. "How's Martine?"

Sharlee smiled, broad mouth and perfect teeth, her face lighting up. "She's great. Got married to a guy who works for a big accounting firm and she's working as a part time teacher. They've got two little boys as cute as can be."

"And your mom?" I asked, further checking her out. She had high cheekbones and a wonderful smooth chocolate brown complexion. Her hair was tied with a small red ribbon in the back then thickly flowed beyond her shoulders.

"Doing good. She moved into a little 'grandmother's apartment' constructed on the side of Martine's house. She helps with housework and looks out for the two grandkids. It works out perfect for all of them."

"But, don't you have a place around here?"

Sharlee's eyes slightly looked down. "It's just been sold. We thought I'd have a job by now and could get on with a career, maybe get my own place. But now I don't know what to do, maybe move in with Martine."

"That's what we are talking and praying about," Clyde said.

"Something's going to work out."

Janie sat there listening, her back up straight. She tugged at her camisole top, pulling it up a bit.

There was movement from the kitchen and Rochelle emerged carrying a tray of cookies. "My, my Hank." She put the cookies on the coffee table and I stood up and we hugged each other, her firm black arms squeezing my chest.

Rochelle was warm and soft and every time I was around her she made me feel good, the only real mother I ever had. I introduced her to Janie, and then Clyde started a conversation with Janie, Jake and Elena.

Rochelle looked at me, and then at the kitchen and jerked her head in that direction, and I knew it was pow-wow time with her. We both went into the kitchen.

Rochelle shut the door behind her and immediately said, "Does she go to church?"

"What do you mean?" I asked, knowing where she was going and knowing she always got straight to the point.

"You know where I told you to find girls."

"She goes to a good school, her family is wealthy and I haven't had any trouble with her, yet," I stated.

"How long have you known her?" Rochelle asked.

"Ah, two days."

"Then you be careful. Now I'm not saying she isn't right for you because I don't know her, but Hank you know I don't want you to get hurt."

Rochelle had spent many hours counseling me on relationships. "I'll be careful."

She looked at me with kind eyes. "I'd advise you to go slowly. Take your time to get to know this girl. She might be the right one and she might not, but it hurts me when you get hurt. You know I love you Hank. And the Lord knows the suffering that Jake went through with that wild woman. You boys have got to be careful."

Her words touched me. Rochelle had always wanted the best for me and she had done so much to help me though that tough time after the Romero Rodriguez incident and the years that followed. She always showed tough love, but it was what I needed.

"I'll try, but she's really gotten under my skin," I said.

"Well I can sure tell you that she sure is a real looker. As you boys would say, she's hot," Rochelle had a big smile.

We went back into the living room and Jake looked at his watch and said, "I think we gotta go."

Rochelle said, "It's so good to have you boys back here with us. Let's have Sunday lunch together sometime. Maybe come for Sunday services."

Jake grinned. He missed it as much as I did. Jake turned to Sharlee and said, "You want to come to a concert with us?"

She smiled. "Thank you, but we have something going on here."

Clyde interjected, "We're going to spend time to talk about Sharlee's future."

"Well, maybe you can join us next time," Jake said.

"I'd like that," she said.

We all stood up and it was then that I saw how Sharlee had grown. She was as tall as Janie, maybe five ten or eleven. She was wearing beige cotton pants and a blue cotton blouse with small delicate pink flowers. I quickly noticed that she was still slender in the waist but had filled out in the right places.

'Nice to see you again Sharlee," I said, "and good luck with the job search."

"Nice to see you too Hank."

We started toward the door, but I turned back for quick glance at Sharlee and caught her looking at Janie, and for a split second her eyes went tight, piercing, *los osos negros*, breathing fire, like a black Latino.

CHAPTER 9

We all rode together in Jake's car and headed south for about a couple of miles deep into the black section of town. It was an area where we felt at home with rows of small businesses, Laundromats, pawnshops, soul food restaurants and liquor stores.

I was in the back seat next to Janie and she and Elena were talking about clothing, what was popular in Europe versus North America. Elena was describing what Ukrainian women wore, how the style was very much like the rest of Europe. I wasn't really listening, as my mind was drifting to Sharlee. It was good to see her again, although that look she gave Janie surprised me.

My mind drifted back to our years at the Baptist church, how Sharlee used to follow me around all the time. She was the cutest thing, full of pep and laughter. Jake used to call her 'Hank's shadow'.

It made me nostalgic for those times, although they weren't always all that easy. For the first couple of years while living with Clyde and Rochelle I was often receiving visits from a Social Services person who was something like a probation officer for juvenile delinquents. Clyde and Rochelle helped smooth all of that, but it still was a difficult time in my life.

Rochelle's cooking, tender loving care, and wise counseling were some of the factors that took off some of the rough edges on a hardened teenager who was out to fight the world.

Jake and I always resisted going to church on Sundays, but in reality we liked the place. The people there became part of a larger family that we never knew. They were warm and accepted us. The services were miserably long, but lively. And honestly seeing Sharlee each Sunday was something I always looked forward to. Just being liked by someone, even swooned over, was an entirely new thing for me. At the time I secretly had the hots for Martine, but now that I thought about it, it was Sharlee who stirred my heart the most back then.

Now, it disturbed me to know she was having a difficult time to find a job. Her family had fought so hard to do the right thing, to study hard, stay out of trouble and to get a higher education. So many young women who grew up in her situation become unwed mothers or went into drugs and prostitution, along with all the other evils you found in the world around here. Martine and Sharlee managed to stay clear of all of that and I admired them for it. I just hoped that some good would come to Sharlee, but I knew there was nothing I could do for her.

Jake parked the car and Janie asked, "Where are we going?" She looked up the street, her eyebrows tight. The street was dark and ominous, a bit like a war zone.

"Over there," he said, pointing across the street at a large wooden building. "Brother's Club. Best music club in L.A.; Jazz, Soul, Rap, you name it. They've even done Country Western if you can believe it."

Janie's face was still, her eyes wide and focused.

Outside the club was a line of people waiting to get in, only blacks.

We got out of the car and went across the street and the bouncer saw Jake and waved. Then he saw me and motioned for us to come to the front door. "Morgan, how you doing brother?"

"T-Row, what's new man? You still got that hard head?" We had been in high school together where we played on the football team. He was known for his illegal, very effective head butts. It was a high school where Jake and I were in a minority and we ended up having to prove ourselves. We told Clyde and Rochelle that our black eyes and cuts came from football, basketball and wrestling, but they really came from the process of gaining respect, two hyper-tough white boys.

T-Row grabbed my hand and we hugged and then he did the same with Jake. "You guys go right on in, but you gotta leave the ladies out here with me." He laughed.

"Yeah, right," Jake said.

We walked through a metal detector where a couple more bouncers were searching people for weapons. A box behind them held an assortment of knives, brass knuckles, a small metal club and I even saw a handgun. As Janie walked through the metal detector I saw T-Row look down at Janie and he gave me a thumbs up.

We went in and behind us I heard someone in the line say, "You give whitey preferential treatment."

T-Row said, "Shut yo mouth. That's Morgan and Jake. Doan mess wit them."

That was all we needed, a reputation before we even went into the place.

* * *

Brother's Club was a large room with a wooden dance floor in front of a slightly raised stage on the far end of the room, and tables and chairs at higher levels around the perimeter like an amphitheatre. Loud rap music blared over the speaker system and the place was already crowded, maybe three hundred people.

"Come on," Jake yelled as he led the way across the room.

Eyes followed us. We were the only whites in the place. Janie had a look of concern on her face. I couldn't tell if it was fear or fascination or a combination. She put her hand on my arm and walked along beside me. I heard some whistles in the crowd.

Jake led the way to a table where two couples were sitting, reserving places for us. The guys were two of our old high school friends, fellow football players, Delay Brown and Rayshawn James. After introducing us to their girlfriends, we ordered drinks and then attempted to carry on a conversation with the loud music.

I looked around the room and saw groups of people talking, laughing, and tapping each other on the hands and shoulders. The body contact among the blacks was much more free and spontaneous than among the whites. Bodies swayed to the music. This is a world that took adjusting to, but these were my roots, along with West L.A.

Around the room I spotted faces I knew, from high school and others I had met over the years. I received nods and smiles. A number of old friends came by our table and greeted us.

Finally at ten o'clock the live music began. They liked to mix up styles in this place, as it brought variety to the show. An up and coming rap group from Watts came on with lots of power and attitude. Their words spoke of the struggle of growing up in poverty and surviving within the system. They really got the crowd into it.

After their third song I saw a group of eight guys come into the room. Two large broad shouldered guys led the way, each of them about six feet six, and I guessed around two hundred and fifty pounds. A smaller guy wearing a white silk suit followed them. He had several long gold necklaces around his neck and gold and diamond rings on every finger. He wore two large diamond stud earrings. Five more guys followed dressed in various shades of purple and black. They followed the guy in white like royalty.

The first guys cleared out some people at a table just off to our right and sat down. All eyes in the room were on them.

Rayshawn leaned over to me and said, "King-Fu."

"The dealer?" I asked.

"Yeah, bad news."

I had heard of King-Fu who ran drug dealing in one section of Watts. He had been considered a small time player, but was now gaining territory. Several gangs were working for him, but he liked to pick young teen boys to do the street work of trafficking drugs. I hate drug dealers because of what happened to my mother and to my friends in West L.A.

I watched King-Fu slowly look around the room. People avoided eye contact with him. He seemed uninterested in the music, but more interested in intimidating people and establishing his supremacy. Then I saw him look at Janie and his eyes fixed there.

Janie was looking at the group on the stage. She was smiling and moving to the music, bouncing back and forth, the camisole top drifting downwards.

King-Fu had a small grin on his face and he locked into a stare partly at me but mostly at Janie.

I kept looking at him and was feeling uncomfortable and wondered if we shouldn't get out of the place, but I knew that I had friends here and shouldn't worry. I decided that we could stay through the live show and then leave.

The rap group ended their performance and another one took their place and at that point I went to the restrooms. Just as I was finished washing my hands and throwing my paper towel into the wastebasket, the two large guys who had preceded King-Fu walked in. I almost thought they were twins, but they weren't.

They stood with their arms folded, blocking the way to the exit door.

"King-Fu want to deal with you," one of them said.

"How's that?" I asked looking at him in the eyes.

"Five thousand for the girl."

I looked at them, both bigger than me and they seemed like a couple of street dogs that had seen their battles. At the same time bulky muscles aren't always that effective. I'd faced bigger guys than me when they made me an instructor in the Marines, but these two guys in front of me were very intimidating.

The first one was standing with his legs evenly spread, too relaxed, and I instinctively knew that was his point of weakness. Without answering I quickly lifted my foot off the ground and smashed it into his kneecap and there was a loud crack as his leg folded backwards. He let out a large "Ohhhh…"

The second one was surprised but he was quick and he took a swing that glanced off the side of my head and I saw a flash and stumbled backwards. He came at me like a bull charging forward but I managed to switch my position stepping sideways and then getting my arm around his head and using his movement to bounce him hard off the concrete wall. He went down and I kicked him in the back and he rolled on his side and attempted to get up, and I got in a solid kick to his head and he was out cold. I went to the one with the broken knee and I grabbed his head and lifted it and began smashing it up and down off the tile floor.

Rage filled me and disconnected thoughts went through my mind; five thousand for Janie, King-Fu can stick it, the injustice of my youth, Romero Rodriguez, the sergeant, my mother and the drugs. Nothing made sense, but in wretched anger I was pounding his head on the floor up and down and up and down.

Hands grabbed my arms and shoulders and I heard a familiar voice.

"Hank, Hank. Stop man. You gotta stop."

It was Jake. He put his arms around my chest and pulled me away. Delay and Rayshawn were there with him, pulling on my arms.

I looked down at the two guys on the floor. "Ass holes," I said.

The one with the broken knee looked up at me with helpless eyes. Blood was flowing from his ear. "You crazy man," he moaned.

I kicked him in the stomach.

"Let's get out of here," Jake said. "Calm yourself man."

We went back into the club where the rap group was still performing. My head was throbbing from where the guy had hit me and the music didn't help. We made it back to our table only something didn't look right. A couple of guys dressed in dark purple were standing in front of it. Others were seated next to Elena and the girlfriends of Delay and Rayshawn. King-Fu was in the middle seated next to Janie. He had one arm around her back and the other was resting on the bottom of her breast. Her eyes were wide open.

Something snapped and I charged forward and hit the first guy I came to on the back of the head and he fell forward without knowing what happened. I could have broken his neck. I didn't care. The guys who were seated next to our women saw me coming and started to get up, but the table stopped them.

I dove across the table directly at King-Fu and smashed downwards with my fist into his mouth and I felt cracking as teeth were dislodged. I hit him again, only this time harder and felt his jaw break. Some of his guys were starting to grab me, and I locked on to the arm of one of them and twisted it while raising my knee and pushing downward, then pulling his arm backward. It snapped.

Jake was on to the guy that was sitting next to Elena, and Delay and Rayshawn were tangling with others. I got lost in a frenzy where I kicked at groins and smashed faces with my fists and bit ears and gouged at eyes with my fingers. I hated drug dealers and wanted them dead.

The rap music came to an abrupt stop and people cleared back from our area and watched. Some of our friends jumped in on our side holding down one guy while Rayshawn kicked into his ribs. One by one we picked them off until I saw T-Row the bouncer swinging a baseball bat. It cracked the head of one of the gang members.

King-Fu was getting up and he had a knife in his hand. It should have been detected by the metal detector at the front door, but somehow he got it through.

T-Row swung the bat and it cracked into King-Fu's head. It sounded like someone chopping on a wood log. King-Fu twisted backwards and bounced off a chair and onto the floor.

The commotion ended and the place was quiet. T-Row announced to the crowd, "Okay, calm down. Weapons aren't allowed in here. Yo'all saw that he had a blade."

The other two bouncers came running and T-Row said, "Some of these guys are pretty messed up. We need to get them to the hospital."

He turned to me and said, "Come on."

We followed T-Row and walked quickly through the crowd. I felt some pats on my back and saw some of my old friends smiling. One of them said quite loud, "Don't mess with Morgan and Jake." Our high school reputation continued, but little did they know that now we were only a lifeguard and a short order cook.

Janie tightly held on to my arm. I felt her hand trembling. The others walked behind us.

We went to a side door, and T-Row started patting us on the shoulders. "You guys can still mix it up."

"Sorry about that," I said.

"Don't worry about it. We don't like those guys coming here anyway and now we have an excuse to keep them away. Entering the premises with weapons."

"They looked hurt," Janie said.

"Not enough," T-Row replied. "

"Will the police get involved? She asked

"Naw, we don't call them in for minor tussles," he said. T-Row turned to us and smiled. "You guys come back any time, but maybe wait a day or two."

I wanted to say something like he doesn't use his hard head any more, rather a baseball bat, but it seemed inappropriate. Instead we just shook hands.

Jake drove us back to get my Jeep and then we all met at a small quiet bar where we had some drinks and let the adrenalin wear off.

Elena was very lively, like she had witnessed something out of an American movie. Jake's left eye was puffed up and I suspected it would be black and blue tomorrow. Delay and Rayshawn acted like nothing happened, two ghetto boys who had learned to just get on with life. Their girlfriends clung to them. From the looks of things I imagined they had something to look forward to later that night.

Janie was quiet, not saying anything, her eyebrows tightened. After about an hour she turned to me and quietly said, "Can you take me to my car?"

I nodded.

★ ★ ★

The drive back to Rodeo Drive was deathly quiet until Janie started to cry. She whimpered to herself, "I can't do this… asking too much."

"What's that?" I asked.

Her head came up and she looked over at me. "It's nothing."

I shifted my eyes over to her and then back on the road ahead. "I really want to apologize for tonight. It just shouldn't have happened."

She didn't answer, but continued to softly cry.

We got back to the coffee shop near Rodeo Drive, but she directed me to the office building with the underground parking lot. I parked in front of the building and went around to her side of the Jeep and let her out, only this time she didn't hug me or kiss me but walked straight into the underground parking.

I drove around the corner and waited, and like the previous night I followed her to the house in Beverly Hills.

And that ended my second day with Janie.

CHAPTER 10

The following morning I was back on the lifeguard stand, a large cup of black coffee in my hand, my head hurting from last night. I felt miserable, not because of the head, but because of me. I just didn't understand why I did those things. It's one thing to get into a fight, especially when you are backed into a corner. It's another thing to let violence overtake one's reason.

Something happens in me where I just want to destroy the world around me, where something is released from the depths of my being for which I have no control. I would have killed the two messenger boys in the restroom if Jake and our friends had not pulled me off them. Likewise when I saw King-Fu with his hand on Janie something clicked in my head and anger took over.

I had a history for this, the fights in high school where I gained this reputation as a tough guy, attacking the drill sergeant in the

Marines, last night at the Brother's Club, Jacko's two gang members...
and Romero Rodriguez. I just wanted to destroy and kill, and this
frightened me.

For two years in the Marines I was a defense instructor and that
taught me a lot, every day down in the pit *mano-y-mano* against recruits.
Most of the time it was straightforward stuff, but once in a while you
got someone who wanted to prove something and then the going got
rough. Most of the time I constrained myself, but once or twice the
monster in my soul took over. I thought I had conquered it, but last
night showed me something different, a personal defeat.

The worse thing about it was how Janie had responded. She cried all
the way back to Rodeo Drive and then she didn't even say goodbye.
Maybe Jake was right; she was just a rich girl that got turned on by a
bad boy. Now that things went way beyond her limits she would go
back to her secure world of rich people's parties, discos, and the family
swimming pool. She had her moment of fun, but it got out of hand
and she recognized the danger. Now she would dump the bad boy.
This only added to my gloom.

So, what could I do? I would do what I always did. Lick my wounds
and suck up my pride and just move on. I had a couple of more weeks
of the lifeguard job, had built up a little cash in the bank, and now I
would focus on TechZip. At least the news from Robert Campbell was
good, that we had a working product. But this news still didn't help
in my introspection of the weakness in my own character and the loss
of Janie.

I nursed the coffee along, expecting a long day. People were arriving
at the beach, putting down their towels, pulling out books, and
applying sun cream. I looked at the spot where Janie had put her towel
two days ago and the image of her came back to my mind. It would
be a long day.

My cell phone rang and I answered.

"Hello, Hank?" It was Rochelle.

"Hello Rochelle."

"What happened last night?"

It was so like her to fire away point blank. "What do you mean?"

"News travels fast in this part of the world. There's some rumors
about a fight over at Brother's Club. It seems that a couple of white
boys involved. That wasn't you and Jake, was it?"

"Ah..."

Before I could answer she said, "Hank, there were four guys that ended up in the hospital. Two of them are in serious condition, one with a broken knee and the other with a broken jaw and some teeth missing. They both have concussions and the one with the broken jaw is in a coma."

Rochelle worked at the hospital part time as a Psychologist. She would know all the details. "The guy pulled a knife and T-Row hit him with a baseball bat," I said.

"T-Row? Your old high school friend?"

"Yes."

"Well, how did this guy lose his teeth and get his jaw broken?"

"Must have hit something when he fell." I held my hand in front of me and looked at the bruises on my knuckles.

"Hank, I don't want you and Jake going back there to the Brother's Club. You hear me?"

"Yes, Rochelle."

"And how is the relationship with the young lady?"

"Not so good."

"Just as well," she said. "You need to find yourself a Christian girl. I pray for you boys every day."

"Okay, Rochelle, I need some help. How do I do it?"

"You know how," she stated her voice ascending, commanding and sure. "See you in church."

She hung up.

I found myself shaking and emotion filled my guts and I felt like crying, but I haven't cried since I was five when my mother died of an over dose. Rochelle's phone call shook me but it actually made me feel better, knowing that someone cared. Rochelle has a PhD in Psychology but when it comes to me there are no subtle psychological counseling techniques. She gets straight to the point. Tough love. I love Rochelle.

Ten minutes later the cell phone rang again.

"Did she call you?" It was Jake.

"Yeah."

"Wow, she let me have it. How about you?"

"Yeah, kinda," I replied.

"That got out of hand last night, didn't it?"

"I know, but we didn't initiate it. We were there to watch a concert."

"But there are four guys in the hospital."

"It wasn't only us. T-Row did his part."

There was silence, and then Jake said, "Hank, I get worried about you sometimes. I wish you could control yourself. It's going to get you into trouble."

I'd already been in trouble because of this weakness, but I understood Jake's concern. "I know. I'll work on it."

"Just please do your best," he said. "Did Rochelle lecture you on women?"

"For sure. What did she say to you?"

"She likes Elena."

"No kidding," I said.

"Elena's a practicing Orthodox Christian and that's okay in Rochelle's book, almost as good as a Baptist."

I laughed. "How did Elena take it last night?"

"She had a great time. Those eastern European girls are tough. Anyway she told Sam and the crew over here all about it. Sam thinks that you and I are American heroes. You'll get free Moussaka for a year." He paused. "How about Janie? How did she take it?"

"Not good. Last night she didn't even say good-bye. It's finished and now I just have to move on."

"Sorry to hear about that," he said.

CHAPTER 11

The day was longer than usual. I had to warn some teenage boys who were dangerously dunking some girls under the water. The surf was up and I had to be extra attentive, especially since there seemed to be more people at the beach than normal. Maybe they were getting in the last days of August before school started.

I had an hour break at lunch and went over to the hamburger restaurant where Janie and I had first talked. I ordered a fish sandwich and lemonade and sat at the same wooden table where we had talked. I guess I sat there because it somehow gave me a feeling of being near her, but it really didn't work. I looked around and realized that I didn't like Malibu. I looked forward to get out of here in two weeks.

I reflected again about what happened last night, about the drive home, how she had cried and about the only thing she had said was something like, she couldn't do this and it was asking too much. Then she wouldn't tell me what that meant. I needed to quit being so introspective and analytical, and think about other things.

Ten minutes before the end of my shift I heard a voice off to the side of the lifeguard hut.

"Hi Hank."

I turned. It was Janie. She looked up at me and smiled.

"Janie," I said.

"You okay?" she asked.

"Well, yeah, I guess. But, how about you? I was worried." She was wearing a tiny red bikini patterned with small strawberries, at least where there was enough cloth to show the pattern. Her eyes were red.

"Don't worry about me. Can we talk?" She asked.

"Ah… sure, but could we wait a few minutes. I'll be off pretty quick."

"Hank, is there a place where we can be alone, just you and me?"

"Well, how about the hamburger stand over there?" I said.

She shifted her weight. "No, I mean to be really alone."

"What about your place at Paradise Cove?"

"There are people there. How about your place at Venice Beach?"

That made me feel terrible. I didn't want to take her there, for her to see my real world. "I can't", I said.

"Why not?"

"I… ah… don't feel it's good enough, for someone like you."

She smiled. "Being with you anywhere is good enough. Let's be alone."

I hesitated and then took out a piece of paper and drew the directions on how to get to my place.

CHAPTER 12

When my shift ended I left Malibu and hurriedly drove back to my place at Venice Beach and tried to clean up the apartment, putting away clothing, washing some dishes and making the bed. It didn't make any difference. The place was sparse and I couldn't do anything about that. Then I showered, put on a clean t-shirt and jeans, and waited wondering what she wanted and how things would go. I had several restaurants in mind in the area and thought we could go directly to one of them, and therefore avoid staying in my apartment.

At seven o'clock she drove her Ferrari through the opening in the fence and parked in the dirt parking lot. I left my apartment, locking the door behind me, and descended the rickety wooden stairs.

She smiled as she got out of the Ferrari. She carried two paper bags, and she handed one to me. "Dinner's on me," she said.

"Well, I thought we could go out. There are some nice quiet places around here."

"Dinner's done. Can we talk? Why waste time?" She handed me one of the bags and I looked inside; Chinese takeaway.

I nodded and we went up the stairs, I unlocked the door and opened it, and we went inside.

She quickly looked around and smiled.

"I know. It's simple," I said. "I didn't have much money when I was working my way through UCLA and the last year was tight."

"Unpretentious, but I like it. The complete opposite of my world."

Somehow that made me feel better, but I was still nervous having her here. She wore a pink blouse with the top two buttons undone and shiny pink shorts in some kind of stretchy material that tightly fitted her form.

From the second paper bag she pulled out two bottles of wine, a red and a white and set them on the kitchen counter. She walked into the small open kitchen and pointed at the cupboards. "Dishes?"

I pointed at one of them and she opened it and took out two plates and she opened a drawer and took out a serving spoon and then served two plates of food from the containers and set them on the counter.

"Can you open the wine," she said.

It took me some time to find my corkscrew. I couldn't remember the last time I had opened a bottle of wine in my apartment. Then I took the bottle of red and started to open it.

"Uh, uh, white first." She pointed to the other bottle.

I shrugged my shoulders and then successfully opened the bottle without breaking the cork.

"Sit," she said.

I took a place at the table and smelled the food and my stomach growled. The fish sandwich at lunch didn't go a long way.

"*Bon appetit*," she said.

I began to eat and asked, "Why?"

"Why what?" She delicately held the fork, pausing in mid air.

"After the past two nights, Jacko's gang and Brother's Club. I thought you were done with me. Last night you seemed pretty upset."

"I guess I was." She put the fork back down.

"Then why are you back here to see me?"

She looked me in the eyes. "I like you Hank. Everything about you interests me, your background, how you react to these… situations, how you worked your way through college, your project, everything. I would like to know you."

Her eyes scanned down my body and I felt a shiver go down my spine. Jake was right. She's a rich girl who is turned on by a bad boy, a temporary toy. His advice was to enjoy it but be careful. I decided to make the most of the time.

We clinked glasses and I tasted the white wine, an Australian Chardonnay that was way out of my league. The smell of it was fruity and it tasted rich and buttery. It went perfectly with the food. I drank my glass half down and she refilled it.

I looked for a conversation topic. "What's your major at Vassar?" Previously she told me she was a Senior there.

"Ah… history, with an orientation toward law; pre-law."

"Pre-law? Wow," I said.

"Well, there's this boy friend who got me interested in it."

"You have a boy friend?"

"Well… no. Back east, he's a lawyer, but it's not important now. It's on hold but finished if you know what I mean? You see he's kinda controlling, or was, so it didn't work… but he still tries to call from time to time."

I was a little surprised. "Is it serious?"

"No. Not at all. It's complicated, but there's nothing to worry about."

This relieved me somewhat, but I wasn't sure what she was really saying. At the same time I didn't want to talk about past boyfriends or girlfriends. If we got into that, then my story would fill a book. I changed the subject. "So do you plan to go on to law school?"

Her eyes shifted away and I saw her looking at the photo on the table of my mother holding me as a baby. "Law school? Yes, I'm thinking about it."

"Where will you go?"

"Haven't decided yet. What are all the papers stuck to the wall over there?" She poured me another glass of wine and some for herself.

"Just some of my project stuff."

"That's interesting," she stated.

"Why's that?"

"Well, I find it interesting that someone would put it on the wall where they live and sleep."

"Helps keep me focused. Most of the important stuff is downstairs in my garage."

She smiled and turned toward me, her leg slightly touching mine. "Oh I'd love to see that."

"Why?" I asked.

Her eyes blinked. "Well, because. You know what I said about people who started their companies in garages. I find it fascinating. I find you fascinating."

"It's not that important," I said. Mainly I didn't want to take her down there. The place was a mess, and I was sensitive about who went into the garage. All my important files were there in binders and on the PC."

"Oh, come on," she said.

I noticed that we had finished the bottle of white and she was opening the bottle of red. I had also been woofing down the food. She took two clean wineglasses and poured a glass for each of us.

She raised her glass and said, "Taste this."

We clinked glasses and I drank the red. I had never had anything like it before in my life. It was heavenly with rich aromas that filled the senses. She placed a hand on my knee and then gently moved it a few inches up my leg.

"What do you think?" she asked.

My head was spinning from the white wine, which was the best I had ever tasted, but now this red was exquisite. Her hand on my leg only enhanced the sensation.

"It's amazing," I said and I drank some more.

She filled my glass again. "I thought you'd like it."

We finished the meal and I couldn't believe that I had eaten everything she had brought, which was abundant. The bottle of red was now a quarter full.

She put her hand back on my leg and said, "Hank. I find you very interesting. Please tell me about your life, your plans. Please show me around because I am interested in how you live, and if you don't want to take me downstairs, that's okay, but it would be nice to know you completely." She looked at me with her gray-blue eyes, bending forward.

"Then what can I tell you?" I said, maybe slurring a word or two.

"Everything."

And I did. I took her down to the garage and showed her where I did my conceptual work and how I controlled the finances and my business plans. She seemed thrilled to be in the presence of "a future

American legend, like Hewlett and Packard." She hugged me and then pulled my face down to hers and kissed me.

And we went back upstairs and on my small single bed. We made love.

And at three o'clock in the morning she drove away in her Ferrari and said, "love yuh Hank," and I found myself saying, "I love you too."

★ ★ ★

That's what happened during my first three days with Janie. And then she just disappeared on me, and a kid almost drowned on my watch, and a male voice kept answering her cell phone.

I reflected on all these things, lying on my bed, trying to understand what had gone wrong. And nothing made sense and at some point I fell asleep.

CHAPTER 13

Brightness was filling my eyes and I opened them and realized it was morning. I was leaning up against a cushion propped up at the end of my bed. Then I saw that I hadn't set the alarm and I was late for work.

I was wearing shorts so I quickly put on my sandals and while running down the steps to my car put on a t-shirt and I broke every traffic law in the book getting to Malibu. Even so, I was fifteen minutes late.

When I got to my lifeguard stand there was another lifeguard there as well as our supervisor.

"I'm really sorry," I said. "The traffic was terrible."

There were worry lines on the supervisor's forehead. "I wonder if we could have a word," he said.

He nodded in the direction of my car and we walked over to it.

He looked at me with worry in his eyes. "I have to be upfront with this, but unfortunately we are going to have to let you go."

His words were incomprehensible. "What?"

"That's right. It has to do with the kid from the surf. Several witnesses claim you were negligent."

"No way was I negligent," I exclaimed. "I saw him go under, pulled him out and followed procedures by the book. Who made the claim?"

He shifted his eyes up and down the street and lowered his voice. "You know this is a tight community here where everybody knows everybody else. Someone important on the city council contacted me this morning and gave me the complaint. He said they would open an investigation unless you left."

Anger was bubbling up inside of me. "Then let them open the investigation. I didn't do anything wrong."

"I know, and I really don't understand it, but the city council guy said they would question the procedures of the entire lifeguard department. My feeling is that we could open up a whole lot of unnecessary proceedings that would be a waste of time and not be good for any of us."

"I don't care," I said.

"Hank, be reasonable. You have two weeks left and then your contract is finished. Why not just take off a couple of weeks early?"

"Then give me the two weeks pay and I'll go," I said.

"Can't do that. The guy from the city council was specific on this. Sorry, but I have to let you go."

My mind was racing to find a solution, but I could see my options were closing. "I'll go if this doesn't go on my record. If it does, then I'll get a lawyer."

He looked at me. "It won't go on your record. We'll just call it early severance. I'll see that you get paid up until today, but please just go and don't make a scene."

I felt like making a scene. I felt like laying the supervisor out cold. I felt like walking into the city council to find the idiot person who set me up like this and smack him silly. But, I got into my Jeep and drove south on the Pacific Coast Highway.

CHAPTER 14

I felt sick to my stomach. Two nights ago Janie expressed her love to me and I had imagined all kinds of things in my mind, like maybe I would move to the town where Vassar is just to be close to her, or maybe we could move in together out here and she could take correspondence courses. And then yesterday she communicates through an intermediary that she doesn't want to see me anymore, without explanation. Then today I lose my job.

My emotions were on a roller coaster ride.

I wondered who was communicating to the influential person on the Malibu city council. Who had complained about the way I had saved the boy from drowning? Surely it wasn't the mother. Then I remembered that there were two guys who were there. Things were happening so fast and I was so focused on the boy that I hadn't really noticed it. They were dressed in street clothing, two guys in their late thirties or early forties, one in a Hawaiian shirt, both in dark pants and dark shoes. Big guys. What were they doing on the beach?

I remembered that the guy in the Hawaiian shirt accused me of taking too long to get to the boy and that I was just sitting on my ass. Yes, I was daydreaming, but I was in the water in plenty of time and actually saw the kid get into trouble, immediately after his mother did.

The other guy, the one in the blue shirt said something like the boy could have died. Well, I did my best and followed procedures and the boy was saved. What right do they have to complain? Yet, there were two of them and they seemed to get the crowd of people on their side, and maybe they influenced the mother? Who were those guys and did they have any connection to Janie? Surely not.

Now I'd lost two weeks revenue that I definitely could've used and I lost Janie. I decided to start with her and see if I could find her, so I parked the Jeep when I got to the turn-in to Paradise Cove Road. It was close to the same place where I had parked yesterday, when I looked down onto her family's property.

I decided to look again.

I knew my way around, so I walked down Paradise Cove Road and then traversed south along the side of a hill along the same path to where I could see the place. Her car wasn't there, but maybe it was in the garage.

I went back to Paradise Cove Road and walked down to the access road to her property. The front gate was open, so I went through and walked to the house. I saw that the surveillance camera turned and followed me.

I knocked on the door and a few minutes later Lola the maid opened it.

"*Por favor senorita Lola. Janie es aqu?*"

Lola's face was stiff and she leaned her head out the door and her eyes shifted across the parking area. "*Ella no está aquí.*" she said.

"*Dónde está? Por favor.*"

"No se. Tal vez en Los Angelas."

"Donde en Los Angelas?" I asked.

"Por favor deje," she commanded.

She begged me to leave and then closed the door. She said that Janie wasn't here and was probably in Los Angeles. I didn't believe her and had to look for myself. I walked over to the garage and opened one of the garage doors. There were three dark Cadillacs in the garage, but no red Ferrari. I shut the garage door and walked along the access road watching the camera follow me.

It took about fifteen minutes to get back to my Jeep and when I got there I could see that something was wrong. The car was tilted a bit, and then I saw that the front left tire had been slashed, on the side of traffic, the most difficult tire to change. There was also a large slash on the cloth top of the Jeep.

On the windshield was a handwritten note: *You don't listen very well. Just get lost or next time it will be all four tires.*

CHAPTER 15

It took a while to change the tire, with cars speeding closely by. I think I understood why they didn't slash all four. Changing one tire meant that I got out of there quicker, but it still left a message. Four tires slashed would have required special help, and maybe they didn't want to risk an angry person going back to the property and raising hell.

I drove to Santa Monica and found a place that sold cheap retreaded tires. While waiting for them to change the tire I went across the street to a hardware store and bought duct tape and managed to tape up the slash in the cloth roof. Just as I was finished my cell phone rang. It was Robert Campbell.

"We got an order." He said.

"We what?"

"You know Unipac? They were in here to discuss that design problem I was working on. I showed them TechZip and they were impressed. They placed an order to try it out. I need to produce some of the wireless readers."

"How many do they want?"

"Twenty."

"Twenty!" I couldn't believe it. I did the calculation in my head, for the software license and then the hardware devices. It was like fifty thousand dollars according to the way Robert and I had priced things.

"I know what you're doing right now," he said. "Stop calculating."

"Robert, that's like fifty thousand dollars."

"Back off a bit. I should have checked with you, but its normal to do a beta test on a thing like this. Unipac was interested and offered to help. It's a golden opportunity. If Unipac signs off on the product, then we have the endorsement of a big name player and that will mean a lot for future sales."

"That's fine," I said, knowing he was right. "Where do we stand?"

"I thought we should just price it a little bit above cost, including some handling charges built in. But, they also agreed to order more if it works."

"What do you mean by handling charges?"

"You just don't make the silly things," he declared. "You've got to handle the order processing, track production, ship them and we need someone on site to support the test."

"I can do that," I said. Now that I didn't have to be a lifeguard I had time on my hands.

"I think it will be bigger than that," Robert said.

"What do you mean?"

"Do you remember how my communications guy was putting out press releases on some target sites?"

"Yeah, sure." I remembered Freddy, the geeky little guy sitting by the computer, but when I thought about it just about everyone working with Robert had that kind of look.

"He's getting some interest from some companies, but he's already loaded with other work. We're going to need some help to do some communications and marketing, and others to do the administration and production."

"Can't you do the production?"

"It's okay for the first twenty, but we are specialists in prototyping, not production. We'll need to find someone to do that. And Hank, I've got another idea, something up in San Jose. Look, is it possible for you to come by the lab so we can talk about this? We need to make a plan."

When he used the word 'plan', somehow that scared me. Robert was more of a spontaneous scientist and his whole lab was anything but a plan. At the same time he had years of experience and he could guide me through the launch of this thing. I told him I'd come by in the afternoon.

After the tire was fixed I drove back to my place with Robert's information going through my mind. It was okay that we were giving a discount to Unipac, but that meant having to hyper-manage our costs. I would be doing that anyway, but now it left little margin for error. I now had several thousand dollars in the bank to help, but we needed to start to generate some real sales with full profit margins, or maybe find some investors.

I wondered how we could achieve all the things Robert had mentioned and didn't see how I could do it on my own. Robert's people could help some, especially with the initial production, but there were so many things to do. And I wondered what his idea was?

As I drove my mind kept switching from Robert's telephone call to Janie and what had happened this morning. Some internal voice was telling me to just forget her, only I couldn't. Maybe Jake was right. Janie was just a rich girl who had used up her toy, threw it to the side, and now goes on to the next thrill.

If that was the case, then I should just lick my wounds and get on with life. But, I thought there was something deeper between us. She mentioned she had been dating someone back east, some lawyer guy, but that it was now finished. Was he coming back into the act? Could that have been his voice on her cell phone? Was he the one who had cut my tire?

At the same time it was difficult to suppress the anger. I wanted to smash everything I saw and held myself back from kicking in my own front door. In my apartment it took me some time to calm down, and then I heard a knock on the door and wondered if one of my crazy neighbors was there to see me about something. I had very few visitors. Somehow I hoped it was Janie. I went to the door and opened it and was surprised to see Martha, Jake's ex-wife.

"Hi Hank," she said. "I was just passing by and thought I'd say hello."

"Jake's not here," I said.

"Oh no, I just wanted to say hello to you. I thought we were still friends. Can I come in?" She stepped right past me into my apartment shutting the door behind her. She was wearing a halter top, low-cut in the front and nothing but skin in the back. Her shorts were so high up that the bottoms of her buns were exposed. She wore thronged flip-flops on her feet.

"Martha, I'd rather not. This isn't a good time for me."

"What do ya mean?" She said.

"Just that. Maybe another time." I remembered the pain she had brought Jake, how he ended up dropping out of the MBA program.

"I was really hoping to get your advice." She walked over to my bed and sat down, legs slightly apart and she put her hands behind her and stretched backward.

"I don't know. I wondered if you ever got lonely?" She asked.

"Sure, sometimes, but not now."

"I was maybe thinking we could spend some time together."

"Martha, I really can't right now. Can you leave?"

"Hank, come-on, maybe just a little fun."

"Martha, another time. Now I've gotta go somewhere." I went to the door and opened it.

She got up off the bed; shoulders sulking and stepped out on the landing above the stairs. I followed her out, blocking the way back in.

She smiled, a funny little grin and then loudly said, "Hank, you're the best," and then she pushed her body up against me and pressed her lips to mine.

It took me a moment to react and she caught me a bit off balance, but I grabbed her around the waist and gently pushed her back. "What's that for?" I asked.

"Because you're my friend," she said.

She turned and happily skipped down the stairs.

Just beyond the opening in the fence I saw a dark car with dark tinted windows. It looked like two people were in the front and I saw Janie in the back, the rear side window down. They had been watching Martha and me. Janie looked at me and I saw that her eyes were red and drawn. Then she looked away and the car drove off and the window powered up.

CHAPTER 16

On my way to Culver City I kept thinking about the look on Janie's face. She seemed as surprised as I was, but there was a look of sadness and disappointment. Did she really think I was seeing someone else? And why was that car sitting out there at that precise time when Martha was in my apartment. I'd wanted to believe that

Janie was coming to see me and that it was just coincidence. At the same time I kept thinking that this was all getting crazy.

As far as the two people in the front of the car, I didn't get a good look at them because of the dark windows. It looked like two men. I got out my cell phone and called Jake and told him what happened.

"Martha's a snake," he said.

"She's never come by before, except when you were staying with me during the time you were getting separated," I said, knowing how difficult this conversation was for him.

"Everything she does is malicious," he stated.

"But why then and was there any connection with Janie? Was it just bad timing, maybe chance?"

"There's never any chance when it comes to Martha. Let me see what I can find out."

"Jake, I don't want you to have to do this. Please stay out of it."

"Don't worry. We've been through worse than this."

"Thanks," I said.

★ ★ ★

Robert Campbell was standing next to a large wooden table holding a circuit board in front of a bright light, intently searching for something. Two of his guys were standing next to him expectantly waiting. I could never tell if the guys around here were direct employees, contract workers, just some of his friends who wandered in, or what.

I waited until he made some suggestions to the two guys and then he walked over to his desk.

He had a big grin on his face when he saw me, and he said, "This Unipac thing is really cool. Let's just hope the product works."

"You've got doubts?"

He laughed. "No way. This thing works, but as I said on the phone there is a ton of stuff to do, besides all the stuff that's coming into Freddy."

"The communications guy?"

"Yeah." Robert pointed in the direction of the skinny seventeen year old that was in his frozen hunch in front of a computer.

"So, what are the plans and your special idea?" I asked.

For the next two hours we discussed what needed to be done. While Robert's lab primarily did prototype development for large technology companies, he had worked with a number of startup companies over the years. He said he liked the diversity and new product innovation that the startups provided. His experience was invaluable to me.

He explained to me that startup companies go through phases and that we had just gone through what he called the conceptual phase, and we were now into the development phase and even a bit the marketing phase. After that came what he called the growth phase. Each phase had its own characteristics and he described them to me in great detail.

One of the important things we needed to do was set up some production operations. We decided to outsource this to a specialized technology company that he had worked with in the past. For now, his team would produce the first twenty products needed by Unipac. We also determined that we needed some administrative and marketing help, although he wasn't sure where we would find it. Getting further financing would also be helpful.

"And your special idea. What is it?" I asked remembering what he had mentioned on the telephone.

"In two days there's a technology fair up in San Jose. It lasts four days. I've got a booth up there with some spare space and I'd propose to use some of that space to highlight TechZip."

"You mean display the product." I wasn't ready.

"Absolutely. All the big companies are there and it would be a chance to visit Unipac, to work out the Beta test with them and also the administrative details."

"And you'll do that?"

Robert laughed. "Not me. You."

"Me?"

"Yeah, you. Four days in San Jose to promote your product. But, you need some handouts and a poster would be nice. If you go, then I'll schedule a meeting with Unipac."

"Then I better get busy," I said, wondering where to start.

"For sure."

I worked through the afternoon and into the evening at Campbell Labs where Robert gave me use of a computer and I started to draft some marketing information. I would go to a printer in the morning to have it made into a brochure. I tried to estimate what this would cost me, as well as the flight to San Jose and the hotel. I booked into the same hotel where Robert was staying. I thought it was expensive, but he said it was run-of-the-mill for the Silicon Valley. He suggested that we share a rental car.

At seven thirty my cell phone rang. It was Clyde.

"Hello Hank. What are you doing right now?"

"I'm working over at Campbell Labs. What's up?"

"Well, there's some bad news. Rochelle just told me. She just got back from L.A. County Hospital. It seems that King-Fu came out of the coma today and some lawyer visited him. It looks like they're going to bring charges against Brother's Club, including T-Row. You've also been named; it looks like civil charges. In other words, they're seeking money for damages and from what Rochelle says, the numbers look big. I mean really big. Can you come over?"

CHAPTER 17

I parked my Jeep in front of Clyde and Rochelle's place wondering what was going on. Today had been a roller coaster ride with my emotions, but by the end of the day my energies were geared up for getting my product launched with Unipac and the technology fair in San Jose. Now this. Just what I didn't need.

I went to the door, knocked and entered. I heard noise in the kitchen, walked in and Clyde was holding a knife and a jar of mayonnaise.

He smiled. "Want a sandwich?"

"Sure, thanks," I replied. Food was always available at Clyde and Rochelle's.

"Rochelle's been over at the hospital all afternoon and is a bit late. I think she's on her way home now, so it's self service around here."

Clyde put four pieces of brown bread on a cutting board and spread mayonnaise and mustard on them. He then stacked them with a generous portion of sliced meat, cheese, pickles, tomatoes, lettuce and onions. He then topped each stack with another piece of brown bread.

"Humble, but it'll help the hunger," he said. He handed me one of the sandwiches and took the other for himself, bowed his head and said, "Lord we thank you for this food. Amen."

"Amen," I automatically said.

"C'mon, sit down." Clyde pointed to the table in the small dining room next to the open kitchen.

He sat in the chair at the head of the table and I took the usual place when I used to stay with them. I felt some nostalgia remembering Rochelle's warm laughter and how she used to baby us.

"Do you have any more information about King-Fu?" I asked.

"Rochelle's on her way. We'll find out when she gets here. I don't know much more than what I told you on the telephone."

"This is all I need," I said. "T-Row said it was a minor tussle, so we left it at that."

"What happened?" he asked.

I told him everything that happened at Brother's Club, and then we moved on to what happened today, how I got fired and then the good news from Robert Campbell and the impossible amount of work that needed to get done to get the shipment ready for Unipac and to prepare for the technology fair in San Jose. I left out the part about Martha coming to my apartment and Janie showing up. I concluded, "This thing about a lawsuit is not what I needed."

"Hank, I don't know what it is about you, but when trouble comes to you it comes in torrents."

There was a knock on the front door and Clyde went and opened it. I heard him say, "Well, come on in. It's good to see you."

A female voice said, "I hope I'm not bothering you. I just thought to stop in to give you an update on my interview today."

"Not at all. Come on in. Have a seat." His voice raised, "Hank why don't you come on in here."

I got up with my mouth full, carrying my sandwich, and went into the living room. It was Sharlee. My heart jumped and I felt happy to see her. She wore a cotton blouse and dark blue skirt, like coming from a business meeting.

"Hello Hank," she said.

I mumbled because of the sandwich. "Sharlee, how you doing? Sorry."

She laughed. "It's okay. The sandwich looks good."

"You want one?" Clyde asked.

"No, thank you. I already had had something to eat, but go ahead."

"Do you mind if Hank sits in?" Clyde asked.

"Not at all."

"So how did it go?" he asked. He turned to me and said, "Sharlee had an interview today with County Social Services."

She described her interview, saying that she had a good contact with department heads she met with. They were friendly, but country budget officials decided to hold back on hiring because of funding issues. They thought that new positions might open up in three to six months and they felt she would be an excellent candidate. In other words nothing tangible.

Sharlee shrugged her shoulders. "It's not easy, but I've got to keep hope."

Clyde reached across and took her hand in his and patted it. "Don't worry, it's gonna be okay."

Her eyes misted up and she ran her index finger below her eyes. "Sorry."

"There's nothing to be sorry about," Clyde said. "It's going to work out."

"I hope so. Things seem desperate," she said.

"There's always opportunity," Clyde affirmed. "Let's just keep looking."

She took a deep breath, nodded, and composed herself. Then she turned to me and asked, "And, you Hank, how are you doing?"

"Oh, you don't want to ask; good news and bad news."

"What is it?" She asked.

"Well the good news is…" and then I got this crazy idea. "What was your degree in?"

She looked up, curious. "Public Administration. Why?"

"Administration. Look, this just came to me. Would you consider taking on a temporary job for a while, at least until you find what you're really looking for?" In the afternoon over at Campbell Labs I had run my numbers. Robert said I needed someone to help and I really needed a jack-of-all-trades, but I also need somebody real quick. There was no way I could pull this off doing it all on my own. I knew that I had enough funding to hire someone at basic wage for a month, maybe two. It meant that I would continue to live on spaghetti, but at least that would give me the bandwidth to get things done.

"What are you thinking?" she asked.

"I need help. Would you be willing to help me out for a month? If you've got job interviews then you just take time off for them, but this would provide you with a little cash and maybe some experience. But I warn you that you'll have to join in with me on a steep learning curve. Things are moving fast. And I warn you that the pay won't be that good at first, until we can generate some sales."

"What is it exactly?" she asked.

"I started this company called TechZip and am being helped by a technology guru called Robert Campbell. We got our first order today, at least for a test of the product, and we need to respond to other companies that are showing interest. I've got to concentrate on the test and Robert has a bunch of other irons in the fire. Robert and I had a talk today and he said we absolutely need someone to handle communications and some administration. What do you think?"

She was silent for a moment and then looked at Clyde.

Clyde raised the palms of his hands and nodded his head.

Her eyes brightened. "Okay."

Clyde let out a big laugh. "I'd never have expected this one. You sure you got money to pay the girl?"

"Just enough," I replied. "But Robert says that's what we need at this point in time and he's got a lot of experience in startups."

I turned to Sharlee. "Is it possible for you to join me at Campbell Labs at eight o'clock tomorrow morning? They are over in Culver City. You can spend the day with me. I've got to prepare some material for a technology fair in San Jose and this would be a good chance to update you on the project."

"Wow, just like that. I'll be there." She shook her head in disbelief.

It was a strange feeling to know that I had my first employee and the thought of it was overwhelming. There was a responsibility there and my mind was racing about the things I would ask her to do with the Unipac order. I almost forgot about the bad news until Rochelle walked through the front door.

CHAPTER 18

Rochelle took her habitual place on the couch next to Clyde. How many times had I seen them there together when they had visitors, or when they were counseling Jake and me? They were a tight two-person team, sometimes a hit squad, unity and diversity.

"Horace Rice came out of the coma this afternoon," Rochelle said.

"Who?" I asked.

"Horace Rice. That's the name of this King-Fu. Anyway, about thirty minutes later a couple of men showed up and insisted on seeing him. Now Mr. Rice was in intensive care and the hospital staff shouldn't have allowed it, but these men were lawyers and demanded to see him. The nurses capitulated, so they went in and talked with him."

"He was able to talk?" I asked. I had this image of T-Row's baseball bat bouncing off his head.

"I guess so, because sometime later the lawyers came out and demanded a private room for their client."

"Who were they?" I asked.

"At first the nurses thought they were your average ambulance chasers, but they were finely dressed, and the ambulance chasers always show up alone, or even send one of their representatives. These guys are based in Hollywood, or somewhere over there."

This confused me. "Why would lawyers from Hollywood be interested in a lowlife drug pusher from Watts? What have they got to gain from that?"

"No idea. All I know is that they are preparing a lawsuit against Brother's Club and I hate to tell you this, but you are also on their list."

The thought of that churned my stomach. "How do you know that?"

"I'm on the staff at the hospital and I have relatively free access to the patients, for psychological evaluation and support, so I visited Mr. Rice."

"And he told you that?"

"For sure. He was extremely talkative. With all the drugs they've been giving him it's almost like truth serum. Only he does have some difficulty to talk because he is missing quite a few front teeth." She looked at me with disapproving eyes.

Sharlee was quietly watching me and somehow her look touched me in a strange way, like a hand calming the sea.

"What should I do?" I knew that whatever it was, I didn't have any time for this.

Clyde said, "Let me ask around in the Social Services. The county has some lawyers available and you may qualify for support, although I'm not sure they would provide anything to a UCLA graduate. But, it never hurts to try."

"Okay, but why do things get so screwed up with me?" I hung my head, feeling lost. A lawsuit would bury me. I didn't have any finances for hiring a lawyer. This whole thing with Janie was driving me insane. I didn't see any hope.

Things got quite and Sharlee spoke softly. "Hank. It'll work out."

I looked at her. Who was she to talk, a ghetto kid without a father who works her way through university, strong enough to confront life's battles, but at the same gentle in spirit; like Rochelle.

"Sometimes I wonder," I responded.

"It's going to be okay," she said.

Sharlee's soft words touched me. It was like a knife going into the depths of my soul. Kids growing up in foster homes are tough nuts to crack and I had impregnable steel walls built up around my being, but being here in this setting somehow got to me. I hung my head and rested my forehead into my hands so that they couldn't see my eyes.

★ ★ ★

On my drive back to Venice Beach I felt somber, beat up, like twenty Marines had kicked the life out of me in the combat pit. I've had some rough days in my life, but this one was high on the list, emotional ups and downs like you wouldn't believe.

A myriad of random thoughts filled my mind and I decided to retrace the events of the day, but circular logic sidetracked me before even getting past the first event. Getting fired from the lifeguard job this morning was a shock, not just losing two weeks of salary, but that someone would even bring this to the attention of an influential city council member. Who was that person and who would have contacted him, or her?

Did those two men on the beach have anything to do with it, the ones in the dark pants? But then again, it was a fact that I had been daydreaming before I saw the kid in the water and maybe my recollection of the events wasn't all that accurate. It wouldn't be the first time in my life that I had misjudged something. Look at how I had messed up things at Brother's Club. With out a doubt there were times when I lacked judgment; like maybe all the time.

Was it lack of judgment that got me involved with Janie? It must have been a real disappointment for her to see me there with Martha pressing her half naked body against me. But what was Janie doing there in the first place? As I drove down I felt an huge void inside my soul, missing her deeply, remembering how we were together two nights ago, the memory of her touch, her perfume, how she made me feel like a man. Yet even here I began to wonder if my reasoning was wrong.

Why was I so obsessed by Janie? There had been other girls. Was it because she the first girl way out of my league that came along? Somehow I felt a personal validation to have someone with that kind of money and looks. Was this my ego play, growing up always feeling inferior, but with her I felt superior? As I thought about it I knew there had been something very special between us the other night, her passionate responses to me as we sought each other again and again, a burning hunger from both of us that was difficult to satisfy. That was the height of personal pleasure and fulfillment, and I knew that I had also met her needs.

Then my thoughts jumped around to Brother's Club and then back to Janie and then what happened in saving the boy, losing my job, and my inability to control my temper. All this made me feel inadequate and then my negative thoughts and self-doubts began to transfer over to my startup project. Who was I to get involved in this kind of business venture?

Maybe I was destined to be a lifeguard all my life, but I'd even messed that up. Maybe I could join Jake as a short order cook? Or, better yet I could team up with T-Row and become a bouncer? But, I wouldn't even be good at that because I wouldn't know where to stop when I was 'bouncing' someone.

My project terrified me. I'd never been in a real business deal in my entire life and here I was dealing with Unipac, a large successful company. They will probably end up laughing at my naivety and inexperience. The best thing for me would be to run away from all of this, to move across the country or to head to Europe or someplace else, or better yet to South America where I spoke the language. And no matter where in the world I would be, there would be a court case hanging over my head in California, because of some evil drug dealer..

And here I was pulling Sharlee into all of this, a beautiful young woman who deserved more than this. I reflected on her upbringing, the conditions of her youth and how her family had been courageous. She must be hurt by my stupidities. Whatever happened, I wanted to do my best for her. At the same time, maybe the best was just to stay away from her. But, I knew that a temporary job would help while she sought something more permanent. At least I could provide that.

So the day had consisted of a crazy jumble of emotion packed events and the only thing I could do was move forward, first with TechZip and then maybe with Janie, although that seemed less and less promising. The only conclusion I could come to was to go ahead and try my best tomorrow to move my project forward. I would do this for Sharlee, and Clyde and Rochelle. If any people deserved the best, they did. At least I could try for them. But, I was carrying a mountain of doubt.

★ ★ ★

I pulled into the dirt parking area next to my garage, turned off the motor, got out my cell phone and called Robert to tell him about Sharlee. I was afraid he would think I was nuts to bring an inexperienced nontechnical person into the project, but he did say that we needed bandwidth.

Luckily he was still in his office and it reinforced my hypothesis that he lived there. I told him who Sharlee was and explained her willingness to help.

He said, "My friend, we are running fast and are at the point where we desperately need some able bodies. You said she's got some kind of degree in administration?"

"Public Administration?" I answered.

"Okay, sounds good enough for me, whatever that degree is. When does she start?"

"She'll be at your office tomorrow morning."

"I like that," he said. "You're moving fast. Startups that hesitate get left in the dust, but several wrong turns in a row can sink a startup. This one doesn't sound like a wrong turn. See you tomorrow."

He hung up.

I went up to my apartment and went to bed, but the crazy jumble of thoughts was racing through my head and I had a fitful sleep. But, I guess it was all part of the mental cleaning process because somewhere in the middle of the night I was back on track focused on my startup company.

CHAPTER 19

At six-thirty the following morning I was in the gym working out and just before eight o'clock I was at Campbell Labs in front of a computer in the small work place that Robert had provided. There were no partitions in the room, total open space. Other guys were there. I couldn't tell if they had arrived early or had been working all night. Things happened here twenty-four seven.

Robert was across the room in his office area seated at a small round table where the same two guys from yesterday were showing him a circuit board. He was explaining something to them.

Things were never really noisy in Campbell Labs, but all of a sudden I sensed that the noise level went down. I looked up and saw Sharlee standing by the door leading to the reception area. All the guys were looking at her.

I waved, got up, and walked over to where she was standing.

"Good morning," I said, happy to see her.

She smiled when she saw me and then she looked around, eyes wide. "What is this place?"

"Geek heaven," I answered.

"It's unbelievable. I've never seen so many wires and random… ah… things."

"You better get used to it. This will be our base for a while, along with my garage in Venice Beach."

"Garage?"

"That's where all my paperwork is and a computer with all my important files." I wanted to say that many important American companies were started in garages, remembering Janie's words, but held back. Seeing Campbell Labs was enough of a shock. "You want a coffee?"

"Yes, please," she said.

I led her across the room and everyone watched us. Robert got there first and was pouring coffee into three cups as we approached.

"Sharlee, this is Robert Campbell," I said.

Robert shook her hand and then his eyes scanned the guys in the room. "This is an all time first. Look at those guys. You're the first woman to ever come into this place. Well, not exactly, but the fact is that this is mainly a guy's hang out."

Sharlee laughed.

We went over to the circular table in Robert's corner office space, sat down, and for the next hour we gave Sharlee an overview of TechZip and the deal with Unipac. Other companies were showing interest in the product. Marketing was needed. We decided that Sharlee's primary role was to communicate with potential clients and handle orders with special attention to be given to Unipac. I would coordinate the test at one of the Unipac sites, as well as work with Robert to outsource production. Robert's team would make the initial production run and would provide technical support until we moved this over to a production company.

"How's that sound?" Robert asked.

"Just fine, but you have to understand that my training is in Public Administration," Sharlee said.

"As long as you know how to turn on a computer, that's okay with us. Right Hank?"

I nodded.

"If you teach me." She laughed. "So, where do we start?"

I said, "Today I'd like you to help me prepare for the technology fair in San Jose. We have to draft some documents and then take them to a printer. This will enable you get to know things a bit better. Then you can answer some emails that have come from potential customers. If you don't know the answers, you can ask Robert or myself."

"Fine. Let's do it," she said.

We worked until eleven on the documents. I already had some drafts and Sharlee and I went through them. She made numerous suggestions on how I could change the wording and even caught a few spelling errors. Somehow it gave me confidence to have her there.

Just after eleven Clyde called me. He did some initial investigations into getting legal help, but I wasn't eligible. He said he would continue to work on it. I thanked him and when I hung up I felt the heavy weight of having to fund a legal case. Where would the money come from.

Sharlee went with me to a local printing company and ordered a rush print job to be completed by the afternoon. It consisted of brochures, product descriptions, and business cards, one thousand of each. The title on my business card was Chief Executive Officer. Robert's was Chief Technology Officer, and Sharlee was Marketing and Administration Manager.

Sharlee thought that was funny. She said, "One day I'm an unemployed college graduate and the next day I'm a manager in a company."

I thought the same. When I legally registered TechZip I gave my title as CEO, but now to actually see it on a business card and knowing that those cards would be given to people was a strange feeling.

I also ordered a large eight foot poster with 'TechZip' at the top and a large blowup of Robert's wireless device receiving signals from computer parts, stacks of shirts and boxes of cereal. Robert said we needed something to grab people's attention at the technology fair and he thought those images would be good in order to show the versatility of our system.

At the top of the poster it said, "Keep Track of Everything", and at the bottom a tag line that said, 'TechZip: Advanced Virtual Inventory Control'.

All this set me back financially. While I didn't order the best quality paper, it was still expensive and I wondered how many other unexpected expenses would hit me. I'd be running out of cash sooner than expected.

After visiting the printer we went to the drive thru at a hamburger restaurant just down the street from Campbell Labs. Sharlee ordered a chicken salad and I ordered a basic hamburger. Then we headed back to Campbell Labs where we would eat our lunch.

As we got out of the Jeep a man approached us. He was wearing a dark business suit, white shirt and dark tie. His clothing looked expensive. He was about six foot with a trim build and his hair was black and combed straight back.

"Are you Mr. Hank Morgan?" he asked.

"Yes."

"Mr. Morgan. My name is Thomas Bennett. I'm from the law firm of Bennett, Medici and Associates." His voice was soft and low-key, like water with no ripples.

"How can I help you?" I asked.

"I probably shouldn't be doing this, but I felt I should advise you to seek legal advice in regards to a claim for damages that is being prepared against you." He smiled, amazingly white teeth, but somehow I imagined a tiger.

"Are you offering your services?" I asked. I wondered if he was contacting me because of Clyde's investigations this morning.

"I represent the plaintiff." His voice was sure and steady.

"Then why do you contact me and how did you find me here?" I asked.

"We found you through our research and I'm contacting you out of courtesy. The legal process will now begin to take its course and you will require representation. I'd advise you to seek an experienced lawyer. This is just to give you fair warning."

"Well, stick it," I said. It was the only thing I knew what to say when being threatened, tough street talk, but immediately after saying it I knew how useless street attitude was when facing the legal system. I'd been through the legal system several times when I was a teenager, getting placed in different homes, some minor infractions, and for the Romero Rodriguez affair, and I knew how cold and impersonal the judges were. Somehow they never seemed to like me.

"That may not be appropriate," Thomas Bennett passively said. "My client, Mr. Horace Rice, is making a significant claim for damages, as his injuries are tremendous. You were the primary perpetuator in the case."

"King-Fu was attempting to fondle my girlfriend's boob." I looked at Sharlee and felt embarrassed and wished I hadn't said that. Her eyes tightened and I couldn't tell what she was thinking.

"We have witnesses that say you attacked him, that is, you ran across the room and started beating him, from which the injuries occurred. There was no cause for this. He was innocently sitting and watching a musical performance." His voice was silky, almost sinister.

"He offered me five thousand dollars for my girlfriend!"

"Mr. Morgan. That's hearsay unless you can produce reliable witnesses. It seems there was a vicious and uncalled-for attack on two of Mr. Rice's friends when they were going to the men's room. Again, I'm kindly advising you to seek the best legal advice possible. My client is severely injured and is seeking considerable financial compensation. You should be prepared to accept this. Now I feel I have given you my opinion out of courtesy. Thank you." He turned and walked over to a yellow Porsche, got in and started the engine.

I just stood there and watched his Porsche pull away. The hamburgers in the paper bag seemed unappealing.

CHAPTER 20

Sharlee picked at her salad as I silently tried to wash my hamburger down with the soda.

"Do you think they have a case?" She asked.

"Who knows what they have."

"What exactly happened at Brother's Club?"

"Nothing. King-Fu and I got into a fight." I couldn't tell her about what I did to King-Fu's two thugs in the men's restroom. I did initiate the physical attack because the odds were not in my favor.

"You mentioned King-Fu having fondled your, ah… girlfriend. Did that start the fight?"

"Yeah, I guess."

Sharlee looked down. "Is she your girlfriend, what is her name?"

"Janie."

"Yes, Janie. Is she your girlfriend?"

I wadded the hamburger wrapper into a ball. "Who knows? She was my date."

Sharlee paused. "Is it serious, with her?"

"It was getting serious between us," I said. At least I would have thought so two nights ago when Janie was lying in my arms. "Now I'm not sure."

"What happened, to make you not sure?"

"I don't know. A crazy chain of events that only leaves questions and no answers."

"Oh," Her eyes drifted down to her salad. "This sounds bad… the court case."

"For sure. I can't figure out why this lawyer showed up here."

She said. "My guess is that he is trying to intimidate you. Lawyers don't do things for the benefit of the person they are suing and I suspect this was nothing more than an upfront positioning to make you scared. They will try and unsettle you in order to get you to agree to the highest compensation possible."

"But, what can they get from me, an old Jeep?"

"Maybe King-Fu just wants revenge. You hurt his pride and his reputation in front of a lot of people. This is a way of reestablishing his authority where he is saying 'don't mess with King-Fu.' That's worth a lot out on the street."

"He's nothing but a damn drug dealer. He shouldn't be on the street." I suddenly wished I hadn't used the word 'damn' in front of Sharlee.

"I know," she said. "I don't like drug dealers. They have done too much harm to our people."

"For sure," I replied.

We let it go at that, as there was no resolve to this. The fact is, I'm facing a court case and don't have any money to hire a two-bit lawyer, let alone a high priced experienced one. And I couldn't even think of where the money would come from for a settlement if it even got that far.

* * *

We finished eating our food and I knew we needed to refocus on the technology fair in San Jose and the beta test with Unipac. As we left the small dining area Robert waved at us to come over to his desk.

We sat down.

"Things are heating up," he said.

If he only knew, I thought to myself. "What's up?" I asked.

"The R&D guys I deal with in Unipac have been talking with some of their division managers. They want to speed up the beta test. Unipac is headquartered in San Jose, so they are asking if you could meet them there. It may turn out to be a one or two day meeting as there are a lot of details to work out. It looks like you may also be having some meetings with a few other companies that have expressed interest in TechZip due to the work that Freddy has been doing."

"No kidding," was all I could say. The confrontation with Thomas Bennett had filled my mind and now I had a hard time to switch it back to TechZip, but Robert was saying that there would be a lot to do on the trip.

"Did you order the brochures and stuff?" He asked.

"Yes, but are they needed? If I'm going to go to meetings, who is going to man the booth?" I knew that Robert already had meetings scheduled with some of the technology companies he contracted with and he was only taking one of his technical guys to manage their side of the booth. The guy was an expert in prototyping and didn't know much about TechZip.

Robert paused, like he was daydreaming, and then said, "This is a golden opportunity for TechZip to gain some exposure and it is important for us to have a representative who can hand out stuff and answer questions." He looked at Sharlee and asked, "You want to go to San Jose?"

"San Jose, what for?" she asked.

"You can help." He turned to me. "What do you think about it?"

"Well, I don't know," I said.

"Think about it," Robert said. "This is an ideal opportunity to promote TechZip at the technology fair, but with you in meetings, who's going to do it?"

I thought about the cost and wasn't sure I could afford it, but Robert did have a point. We needed to capitalize on the opportunity. I smiled. "Yeah. Great idea." I turned to Sharlee. "Can you come?" Somehow I also sensed that having her there would give me some moral support and right now I needed as much of that as I could get.

"But what do I really know about TechZip?" She asked.

"You'll learn," Robert said. "You already know something. We'll just need to give you some basic scripts and you'll do okay."

"Anyway, as our Marketing and Administration Manager., you should be there," I remarked.

She laughed. "Well, I guess. For how long?"

Robert said, "We fly in tomorrow, get set up and it starts in the afternoon, Thursday afternoon to Sunday afternoon, just four days. It's short, but thousands of people from Silicon Valley and other places come to this event."

"Sunday?" She asked.

Robert glanced at me then at her. "Do you have plans?"

"Well, yes, but I can rearrange things." She smiled. "Yes. If it helps I'll do it."

Sharlee and I worked through the afternoon and I tried to give her as much information about our product as possible, its functionality, the benefits, its advantages in terms of other products out there, in what environments it worked the best, and where we saw some of the limitations, as we didn't want to over-hype it. I booked her on the same flight as Robert and me, leaving at nine o'clock in the morning from Los Angeles International Airport.

At five-thirty we left Campbell Labs, as I needed to get over to the printer and pick up all the material. Sharlee said she would meet me at the airport at seven. When I got to the printer everything was ready. I put all the boxes in my Jeep and drove back to my place at Venice Beach picking up a cheap takeout pizza along the way.

Somehow going back into my apartment felt strange. It was only two nights ago that Janie was here, yet with all the things that had happened it felt like it was weeks ago. At the same time, the image of her on my bed stayed in my mind.

I ate the pizza and went downstairs where I repacked all the brochures and printed material into a large suitcase, as well as some in my carryon bag, in case the airline lost the suitcase. Then I went upstairs and packed some clothing for the four days including the one suit I owned. I had bought it when I was the best man at Jake's wedding and hadn't worn it since then.

I set my alarm for five. L.A. International Airport wasn't that far from Venice Beach, but the traffic in Los Angeles is unpredictable, so I planned to get out quick in the morning.

Just as I turned out the light, my cell phone rang.

"Hello Hank."

It was Janie. My heart jumped. "Janie. Where are you? What's going on?"

"Can we talk?" she asked.

"Yes, go ahead," I said. It felt good to hear her voice.

"No. I mean can we meet sometime."

"Now?"

"Now's not a good time. What about tomorrow?" she asked.

"Janie, I want to, but I can't. I'm going to San Jose tomorrow."

"San Jose, what for?"

"I'm going to be promoting TechZip at this important technology fair."

"So, when are you back?" There was some kind of techno music playing in the background.

"Sunday evening."

"Can we meet then?" she asked.

"Yes, for sure. Anytime, but what's going on. Who was that on your cell phone when I called the other day and where have you been?"

"Hank, are you seeing that girl?"

"What girl?"

"The one you were kissing on the steps outside your apartment."

"No, not at all. I don't know why Martha did that."

"Martha? Look, I hope we can talk before I leave to go back east."

"Why not now?"

"I can't. I'll explain. I gotta go, really. I'll call you."

"Please Janie, wait."

"Hank, I can't. Bye." She hung up.

Adrenaline was pumping through my body. I didn't know what to think. She seemed stressed, but she wanted to see me. If she had insisted I would have delayed going to San Jose just to see her, to find out what's going on, and to explain that I'm not seeing Martha.

I hardly slept with my mind going through endless circular logic thinking about Janie. I couldn't figure it out. She first said he urgently wanted to see me and then when I told her about San Jose it was like she immediately changed her mind. What was going on?

She's making me think like an idiot.

CHAPTER 21

We made it to the San Jose Convention Center and it only a couple of minutes to set up our TechZip exhibit. Then Sharlee and I helped Robert unroll a long white canvas banner with blue lettering. It said, 'Campbell Labs: The Super-Geeks who make things work when you can't'. The banner was frayed around the edges and looked like had been used many times before. Actually, Robert didn't need much publicity. He had been around the technology circuit for years and already people from other exhibits were passing by and greeting him.

It felt strange to be here and it made me feel small and insignificant, especially when I saw how elaborate some of the other exhibits were. There were electronic products displayed of every size and shape. Large TV screens were showing fancy video presentations with colors flashing and music blaring from speakers. All the other exhibits seemed to have large posters with logical flowcharts, descriptions, and images, all intended to capture the attention of attendees.

My poster was smaller than most of the others and it was drab, even confusing with the images of the electronic parts, cereal boxes and shirts.

"Don't worry," Robert said. "You've got a killer product. That's what matters."

I had my doubts, wondering if I made a mistake by spending all the money for Sharlee and me to get up here. Who would even take an interest? But in my heart of hearts I knew that the TechZip technology would benefit many different kinds of companies.

We had just got the poster put up when a guy stepped into our area. He asked me, "Are you with TechZip?"

"Yes, can I help you?"

"I'm looking for Hank Morgan and Robert Campbell."

"I'm Hank and that's Robert," I said, nodding in the direction of Robert who was trying to get rid of the sag in his long banner. I called him over.

He said, "My name is Ron Stevens and I work for Unipac. We have a meeting scheduled with you tomorrow, but we have a slight problem in that one of our managers has an unexpected meeting in Seattle tomorrow. He only has a couple of hours today, actually only this early afternoon. So, we're wondering if it is possible for you to come over today, even now, if possible."

My suit was in the back of Robert's rental car and I was wearing beige cotton pants and a short-sleeved sport shirt.

"Who is it?" Robert asked.

"Graham Hodge, the director of one of our divisions.'

"Graham! Sure I know him," Robert said. He turned to me. "Let's go."

"Sure," I said, not feeling so sure. I turned to Sharlee and asked, "You going to be okay?"

She laughed. "I'm a big girl. I'll just hand out brochures and talk with people. You and Robert just go on and I'll see you later."

As I walked away I turned back and she nodded and smiled at me like everything was going to be fine. It gave me some degree of reassurance, but I wished I could have worked with her a bit before turning her loose on her own.

We followed Ron Stevens out to his car and he drove us about twenty minutes to a business park full of square flat roofed buildings. I wondered if we were appropriately dressed, as I didn't have time to put on my business suit. I wanted to ask Robert, but didn't get a chance. Robert didn't seem to be worried about anything.

Ron led us into a conference room with a long oval table surrounded by twelve chairs. Flip charts and a white board were at one end of the room. After a few minutes of waiting a man walked into the room that looked to be about the same age as Robert.

"Hey Robert," the man said. "Long time no see. How's it going?"

"Graham, you're looking good."

They shook hands and then Robert introduced Graham Hodge to me.

"Thank you both for coming," Graham said. "I was scheduled for the meetings tomorrow, but got this urgent thing in Seattle. We are trying to finalize a deal with a large customer up there and it looks like we have to resolve a couple of things before we can move forward. I figure we can fix it pretty quick, and therefore have to fly out this afternoon. Hope you don't mind?"

"Not at all," Robert said.

"So my R&D guys say this product of yours is pretty special. What can you tell me about it?"

We spent an hour with him describing how TechZip worked and then some production managers came in and joined us. Graham left, but we continued on with the production managers, and then a manager responsible for the entire inventory in the factory. Finally at six o'clock Ron Stevens drove us back to the technology fair.

When we got out of the car I asked Robert how he knew Graham Hodge.

"Some years ago it was one of those deals where they came to me for technical help. They were under a tight schedule to release a product, but couldn't get a circuit to work. I fixed it pretty quick. In fact, that's where Unipac became one of my best clients and they opened the door for some other companies."

I knew that Robert had a busy schedule here in San Jose. I said, "You didn't have to spend all afternoon helping me, but I really appreciate it."

He laughed. "Just remember that I am a twenty percent shareholder in TechZip so have a vested interest to make it successful. Anyway, I needed to participate on this one. Graham carries a lot of influence in Unipac and you don't get an opportunity to meet with someone at his level every day. Tomorrow is more about the nuts and bolts of running the beta test. I'll be with you in the morning, but not the afternoon. I need to get back to the fair for some meetings, and I've got some tonight."

We went back into the exhibition hall and went to our space. There was a small crowd of people there and in the middle was Sharlee. She was laughing with someone, carrying on a conversation.

As we approached the stand I saw that she was talking with a gray haired man in a plain blue short sleeved shirt and beige pants, just about the same color as mine. He handed her his business card and I heard him say, "That sounds like a mighty fine product. I wish you good luck."

She gave him one of her business cards and he walked off. Several people walked off with him seeming part of his entourage, whereas others stayed behind and talked with Sharlee. Some seemed to be genuinely interested in the product. Others looked like they were more interested in her.

"You know who that man was," Robert said.

"No, never seen him before.

"That was Sam Oliver."

"Sam Oliver! I read about him in business school. He's a legend in Silicon Valley. He's the founder of Unipac, like a multi-multi billionaire. His son-in-law, Paul Kent, is now the CEO."

"That's him," Robert said. "In living flesh."

"And he was talking with Sharlee!" I was amazed.

"It looks like it."

* * *

We stayed on for another hour and it looked like Sharlee was just getting into full swing. She seemed to talk with people so effortlessly, in fact, much better than me. To be in social situations always made me uneasy and standing there and talking with strange people was not my thing.

Just before closing time at 8:00PM, Sharlee came over to me with a large stack of business cards and handed them to me.

"What's this?" I asked.

"I exchanged business cards with all these people."

I laughed. "Were they interested in TechZip or in Sharlee?"

She smiled. "Some are serious inquiries and who cares about the rest. Maybe we can put them all into a database and send them further information about TechZip."

I shook my head. "That's only day one and it was only half a day. How many do we have here, a couple hundred?"

"Something like that," she said.

"Great job," I said. "I'm impressed." I hoped that some of these would create actual orders for TechZip. All day my cash position was worrying me, and the threat of this court case was not helping that concern.

"You know. It was actually fun," she said.

A man in a dark business suit walked up to us and said, "Are you Hank Morgan?"

"Yes. How can I help."

"My name is Al Manchini and I'm with BMP Capital, a venture capital firm with offices in Silicon Valley and several other places around the country." He was overweight and his belly pushed out against his white shirt. I guessed that he was around forty-five. He handed me his business card and the address was Page Mill Road in Palo Alto. I know that was the street where many famous venture capital firms were located.

He looked at Sharlee, maybe a bit too long, and then turned back to me. "As this technology fair is a place for networking, our company uses this as an opportunity to contact interesting companies. We've heard some positive things about you and wonder if you would be willing to explore how an experienced VC firm can work with you to accelerate your business development."

I had seen one aisle in the trade fair with a number of VC firms that were exhibiting, but not BMP Capital. I thought a moment and knowing I understood little about how this worked, it wouldn't hurt to find out. "Yeah, I think that would be interesting. Are you here tomorrow?"

He looked around and said, "Looks like things are closing here. What are you doing next?"

"You mean tonight?"

"Sure, tomorrow will probably be busy for you and I'm wondering if I could invite you and your colleague here out for dinner, nothing fancy, but you're both probably hungry. And, there's no strings attached. I'd say that we try and keep it short, but I'll try and give you an overview of how things work. How about it?"

I looked at Sharlee and she nodded her head.

I said, "Well, that's very nice of you."

"Then let's go. Do you want to ride with me?"

CHAPTER 22

Our original plan was to take a taxi back to our hotel, as Robert had the rental car. We decided to ride along with Al Manchini in his top of the line Lexus. I chuckled when I thought of the difference between this car and my old Jeep. He drove a few miles and stopped in front of a restaurant where a couple of valets were waiting. They opened the car doors on both sides. I think that for Sharlee and me it was an all-time first.

In the restaurant the maitre-d wore a white tuxedo jacket and black pants and led us through a room full of round tables covered with lily-white tablecloths. We came to a table set with shinny pink and ivory colored porcelain, several shapes and sizes of glasses and a bouquet of small roses. They weren't plastic.

I felt out of place here, underdressed and I wondered if Sharlee felt the same. A waiter brought us a menu. Everything was in French with a translation into English in small letters below the French.

Al smiled, his teeth as white as the tablecloth. "Take whatever you want, but I suggest the *Fois Gras de Canard* as a starter and the *Cotlettes d'Aneau* for the main course. It's pretty good."

That's what we all ordered, "To simplify things for the cook," Al laughingly explained to the waiter. He also ordered a bottle of red Bordeaux wine, although Al and I were the only ones to drink it. Sharlee went with mineral water.

It was the first time in my life that I had ever eaten duck liver and I couldn't ever remember eating lamb. Both were heavenly. I savored every bite and had a difficult time to stay tuned to Al, who did most of the talking. Most of the time he was talking about different deals where BMP Capital had been involved, how much money people had made, and what they had done with it. One guy who sold his company bought a large yacht and just took off to spend the rest of his life sailing around the world. Another one bought a vineyard in Tuscany and an apartment in New York City. Portfolio managers manage their money and they just spend it.

Al said, "These guys have become masters of their own soul, both financially and spiritually, and BMP Capital helped them get there."

I was interested.

Sharlee seemed to enjoy the meal, but when Al said this she sat up straight and her eyes slightly narrowed. "Master of your own soul? Isn't that dangerous. What would the world look like if everyone was the master of his or her own soul."

"Huh?" Al asked.

"The world would become absolutely chaotic." She stated. "Basic philosophical question of where order comes from."

"What?" He paused, a quizzical look on his face. Then he laughed. "I don't know a damn thing about philosophy, but only how to make people rich. What I'm trying to say is that BMP Capital helps startup companies become successful."

"What does BMP stand for?" She asked.

Al looked at Sharlee and I saw his gaze shift down to her blouse and then up to her eyes. "Business Management Partners. You know the crazy way company names get put together, anyway what I was saying is that BMP Capital helps entrepreneurs achieve their dreams."

"Can you be more specific?" I asked, remembering that we covered venture capital as a topic in one of our finance courses at UCLA.

"Well, first and foremost we provide the capital needed to advance your project and that will come in several rounds with more money being injected as the operation grows." He paused for a moment. "What I'm talking about is all the money you need to handle any contingencies whatever they are, without worry. We are a bit more liberal with this than other VC's, because we do everything possible to support the entrepreneur so he can fully focus on his project."

Somehow that sounded good to me.

He continued, "But, we also help in other ways. For instance we have lots of connections. If you need a banker, we can get you one. If you need personnel, we can help with the search. If you need a place to live, we'll supply it. If you need a lawyer, we can get you the best." He took a sip of wine. "And because we are investors in so many companies, we can get them to buy your products. In other words, you can achieve immediate sales. You can have positive cash flow from day one.”

I thought for a moment and asked, “What if the entrepreneur needed a lawyer, but it wasn’t for the direct needs of the company, perhaps for something personal. Would that work?”

“What do you mean?” Al asked.

“I’m just speaking hypothetical, but if the entrepreneur had a personal problem, like someone was suing him for something not directly related to the company, could BMP Capital help?”

Al looked at me. “Look Hank. At BMP Capital our objective is to make the entrepreneur successful, whatever that takes. His interests are number one and we’ll do anything to give him smooth sailing to achieve his goal. Legal help in any form is part of the package.”

I looked at Sharlee. Her head was slightly tilted to one side, her eyebrows drawn.

“May I ask how much capital the entrepreneur would receive in the first round?” I asked.

“That entirely depends on the value of the company.”

“Well, how do you calculate that?”

“Let’s use an example. Your project. How long have you been working on it and how much money do you have invested in it?”

“I’ve had the idea for about six years.”

“No, how much full time work has gone into this?”

“Personally I’ve worked about a year on it,” I said. Then I thought about the work that Campbell Labs had done. “Oh yeah, some software and hardware engineers have helped put together the prototype.”

“Do you have any real orders?”

I thought about Unipac. This was a beta test, so I couldn’t tell him this was a real order. “Just some interest from a company.”

“Well, its when you get real orders that your company will start to take on significant value. Until then it’s valued according to your actual accrued expenses, plus some goodwill. So, based on what you say, we would probably value your company at a hundred thousand dollars for the physical work you have expended, and with goodwill we would top it up to two hundred thousand.”

I felt shocked. My company was worth two hundred thousand dollars! “How long does it take to receive the money?” I asked.

Al laughed. “If you go to other VC’s it will take you two or three months to do it. We’re different. If we like the entrepreneur and have a good feeling for the project, the due diligence will happen quickly. Not much time at all. You'd have the money in just a few days after signing the contract along with all the other kinds of help I mentioned."

That money would really help. For the past few days I'd been carrying a lot of worries, and one of them was how I was going to finance TechZip, and now that I had an employee, the burden was heavier.

"What does BMP Capital ask for this?" I asked.

"Just to be a partner. We want to help. As we figure your company is worth two hundred grand and we inject two hundred, then we would come in as equal partners, in other words, we share the risk with you."

I thought that sounded logical. "Then, where would we take it from here?"

Al laughed. "Now, let's not rush it. The first thing we ask is to sign a Non-Disclosure Agreement. This basically says that we will not give away each other's secrets, nor circumvent each other. In other words everything is confidential and we just deal one on one in an exclusive relationship."

"Exclusive?" I asked.

"Its just a basic memo of understanding, standard boiler plate used in Silicon Valley. You're free to engage with us or not, but we would like to have the privilege to be the first in line to negotiate with you."

"I guess that's reasonable," I said. I knew that Non-Disclosure Agreements, NDA's, were a common tool in the startup company world. Anyway, Robert Campbell said I should always get a signed NDA before sharing any details on my project. In fact, I realized that we should get Unipac to sign one when we meet with them tomorrow.

Al said, "I've got our standard NDA out in the car if you're interested. Want some dessert?"

Sharlee shook her head. I didn't either. I was full from the first two courses. Al paid the bill and we went outside and one of the valets brought the Lexus. We got in and Al reached across to the glove compartment where there was a uniform stack of folded papers.

"Got these things by the gazillions, standard boilerplate NDA. Everyone in Silicon Valley carries these things." He handed me one.

He drove us back to our hotel and there was enough light so that I was able to read the document on the way back. It looked just like the ones that Robert had given to me, very basic. It outlined that we would keep each company's information as confidential and that BMP Capital had exclusive rights to be the sole source of financing to "The

Entrepreneur" until both parties agreed to discontinue the agreement.

When we got back to the hotel parking lot he turned off the engine and said, "How's the NDA?"

"It looks okay to me. So after this we can move forward with the due diligence?"

"That's right. We can start tomorrow."

"How about Monday, as we've got our hands full with the technology fair. Is there a problem that I'm based in Los Angeles?"

"None whatsoever. We have an office down there and I could even come down and manage the process just to keep continuity between us."

"Okay, I'm all in favor of moving fast," I said.

He handed me a pen and two NDA's. I filled in the blanks and then signed my name at the bottom on both of them. Al did the same and we each kept a copy.

He shook my hand and said, "Just remember. We're here to help in all the ways I mentioned, financial, legal, whatever. Let's make you successful. See you Monday."

He turned his head to the backseat where Sharlee was seated. "Oh, and if on the weekend you and or the lady here would like a tour of the sites in the Bay Area I'd be very pleased to show you around."

"We'll let you know," I said.

Sharlee and I walked to the hotel lobby and I was thinking about the money and support that could come from BMP Capital. That would be so helpful. The funding meant that I could pay for marketing and salaries just to jumpstart things. And one thing that I really needed was legal support. If I could get this King-Fu thing off my back it would really help. Let someone else deal with that slithery Thomas Bennett.

In the lobby I turned to Sharlee and said, "What do you think?"

"Do you trust him?" she asked.

"What do you mean?"

She looked me in the eyes. "There's just something there, the insincere smile and smooth talk, 'money-money-money'. It's manipulative."

"That's just how these VC guys are," I said. "They're always making deals and money is central. They just talk that language."

"So, do you really think they're doing this for your good?"

"Sharlee, the best kind of business is where everyone becomes a winner. I win and they win. There's nothing wrong with that."

"I'm not sure," she stated.

"Well, that's how it works." I was getting angry.

"I'm not sure. Do you think they care if you win?"

"I have to win, otherwise they get nothing."

"I'm not sure."

"Why do you keep saying that?"

"Because I'm not sure." Her eyes had attitude.

"Well what do you know about business?"

"Hank, don't sell your soul."

She turned and strode to the elevator, back straight, chin up. She pushed the button, the doors opened and she entered. As the doors shut I saw her looking at me, eyes narrow, shaking her head.

CHAPTER 23

In the morning I didn't go down to breakfast, but just made coffee from the coffee machine in my hotel room. I didn't go because I wanted to avoid Sharlee. Her words last night made me upset, and anyway, who was she to talk to me like that. I had done her a favor by giving her this job. And as far as BMP Capital, what did she know about these things?

Yet, her doubts last night caused me to think. Maybe I was rushing this thing, basing my actions on the personal pressures that had been mounting. At the same time, what Al said had made sense. He knew about company valuations and how to help entrepreneurs. BMP Capital seemed to have plenty of success stories, at least according to Al.

I wondered how I was going to handle Sharlee today. Was she going to sulk because I had offended her, coming down on her knowledge of business? It was true that she didn't know much. Her education was in Sociology and Public Administration. At the same time, she did grow up in the tough part of town and because of that she had street smarts. Maybe there was something to what she was saying. Maybe I should listen to her.

My words last night made me feel guilty. For as long as I could remember Sharlee was kind to me and wanted the best for me. "Hank's shadow," as Jake used to call her. I hadn't seen her for several years, yet she seemed the same. She had a gentle and loving character but with spark, not afraid to speak her own mind. Last night was an example when she got angry with me when I challenged her on her doubts.

But, I had made her angry. Hank's shadow had grown up and now had a strong will of her own. I guess she always did. She always knew what she wanted. At the same time I knew she had expressed herself that way not to get back at me, but because she cared for me.

She was like a little sister, or at least that's how I used to think of her. Now I saw all the men turning their heads and checking her out when she walked by. That made me uneasy. The last thing I want is to see her get hurt. I determined to be more careful in what I say and do around her.

I drank my coffee alone in my room knowing I would have to face Sharlee in a few minutes and then we would begin our day. I planned to first go to the technology fair and then head over to Unipac with Robert. She could hold down the fort at the exhibition, it certainly seemed she did a good job yesterday, collecting all those business cards, getting leads, even talking with Sam Oliver. That was really incredible. She was right at ease with one of the most important men in Silicon Valley.

My cell phone rang and I answered.

"Hello Hank."

It was Janie. I remembered the smell of her neck. "Hi."

"Where are you?" She asked.

"San Jose."

"How's it going?"

"What's up Janie?" My heart felt torn to hear her voice.

"I'm concerned. I just wanted to know how you're doing."

"A few nights ago I was doing well and then a man answers your phone and says you don't want to talk to me. So, how do you think I'm doing?" I could feel the hurt coming back into my soul.

"Hank, it was meaningful to be close to you like that and I thought we had something going."

"Then what happened?"

"I said I don't want to tell you over the phone. I'll see you on Sunday."

"It'll be late. The technology fair ends at five. It'll take some hours to get back to L.A."

"It doesn't matter. Shall we meet at your place?"

When she said that my stomach felt light. I knew what that was likely to mean. "Okay."

"Are you alright? How's it going up there?"

"Good. I might have found some funding for my project."

"That sounds good." Her voice perked up. "What happened?"

"I met this venture capitalist who seems interested. We plan to start the due diligence process on Monday."

"Oh Hank, that's very good. You should definitely go for funding."

"My ah, colleague up here says I should be careful."

"What colleague?"

"Do you remember the girl who was at Clyde and Rochelle's when we were there?"

"You mean the black girl, kind of dressed simply?" Janie asked.

"Ah, yeah, Sharlee."

"Yes, I remember her. You hired her? What did she say?"

"Well, she suggested being careful."

"Careful about what?"

"To not trust the VC."

Janie laughed, more of a mock. "She looks like someone who has never had money, so she probably doesn't know what she's talking about. You know it takes money to make money. Opportunity doesn't knock on the door every day, so you should take advantage of it. I'd say that you should not listen to her, but go for it."

"I guess."

"No, you should. Listen, I think this is great news about this VC and we should celebrate. I'll bring a bottle of Champagne when I see you on Sunday night, and I'll… wear my special perfume." Her voice slowed, soft and sensual.

I recalled images and the scent of her on my bed. "That would be nice."

"Then bring me good news," she said. "I gotta go."

"Me too. I need to get to the technology fair."

We hung up but her soft voice stayed in my mind.

★ ★ ★

We met in the lobby. Robert held his wrist in the air and tapped his watch.

"Sorry, but I received a phone call and it took longer than expected," I said.

"We're late," Robert, said. His technology guy, Matt Sanford was next to him, Sharlee on the opposite side.

Sharlee looked at me and smiled, warm like the morning sun. "Good morning," she said.

"Morning," I said.

I thought of what Janie had said on the phone about the 'black girl who dressed simply.' It wasn't Sharlee's fault that she didn't have the money to buy fancy clothing, and did it really matter? Sharlee's character made up for all the expensive clothing in the world. She was beautiful both inside and out and I didn't think it was fair to put her down like that.

Robert waved his hand in the direction of the front doors of the hotel and said, "Let's go."

We walked to the parking lot, no one saying anything and then go into the rental car and Robert drove to the technology. We went inside and setup things for the day.

Then we left Sharlee and Matt Sanford and went over to Unipac. The rest of the morning we worked with three of their guys going through the details of the beta test. The test would take place at one of the Unipac factories in Los Angeles in order to be close to Campbell Labs where we could give technical support if needed. My job was to test the installation of the system and then train the users on how to use it. We decided that Robert's people would go in tomorrow, install the software and make sure that everything was functioning properly. I would base myself at the Unipac factory starting Monday morning.

The meeting with Unipac was an entirely new experience for me and I was extremely thankful Robert was there. We broke for lunch and then Robert had to get back to the fair while I continued with the Unipac people to discuss some details concerning orderfulfillment and administration. Robert thought it would be helpful to have Sharlee attend so he called Matt Sanford over at the fair and asked her to come to Unipac by taxi.

After lunch we went back to the conference room where Robert gathered his papers and I used that time to update him on the dinner last night with Al Manchini.

"These guys sound serious, although I've never heard of them," he said.

"They have offices on Page Mill Road in Palo Alto, in L.A. and other places," I stated.

"Did they discuss any terms and conditions?" he asked.

"Only in general terms. Mainly he talked a lot about all the ways that they helped entrepreneurs become successful." I thought of the offer of a lawyer.

"Sales hype."

"I know, but we did sign an NDA and they would like to start due diligence next week."

"Already? That's fast."

"They said they move very fast. The capital would be there in a week."

He whistled. "Wow, that's really fast. Never heard of that before. What was in the NDA?"

"Standard boiler plate for Silicon Valley." I tried to sound convincing.

"Do you have it?"

"Sure." I went to my briefcase, took it out and handed it to him.

Robert quickly looked through it and said, "We may have a problem."

"Why's that? It just a normal NDA."

"Uh, uh. Just one little clause here." His finger pointed to a small paragraph at the bottom. "This says you can only deal with them."

"What do you mean?"

"Exclusivity."

"We talked about that. They get first rights to talk with me. I thought that was okay."

"First and only rights."

"Only rights?" I asked.

"Exclusive. Until this NDA is annulled with the agreement of both parties, they are the only venture capital company you can deal with. In fact, even if you go to a bank and ask for a loan, that might be construed to fall under this agreement. In other words, they've got you locked in. You can't get any external financing except through them, and of course that gives them power in terms of negotiating the contract."

My heart sunk. "Then it's either them or nothing."

"Looks like it."

"I can't believe I've done this."

Robert laughed. "Join the club. All entrepreneurs who are starting out for the first time make a number of boo-boos. You're looking at one."

"You?"

"Yeah. I signed contracts, engaged with suppliers and partners and did all sorts of stupid things. It's a wonder Campbell Labs is still alive. Look, next time you have an offer to get into bed with someone, please come and talk with me first."

"Thanks," I said. "But, what do I do with this one?"

"First of all, it limits our options. The only choice now is self-financing, which isn't such a bad thing. Fewer players coming into the deal means that the share capital isn't being diluted, that is, our shares remain intact. When you bring in an outside investor, there are more people who own the pie and your piece becomes smaller. The downside is that your financial flexibility is restricted and you are faced with growing the company more slowly. But then again, I've seen many entrepreneurs get into all sorts of problems when they get outside cash injections. Fiscal prudence goes out the window."

Robert was lecturing, but his words made sense. I held the NDA in the air. "What should I do with this thing?"

"Call up this Al guy and tell him that you want to hold off on the due diligence. If he immediately brings up the exclusivity clause, then you know that you have someone who intends on playing hardball. In that case, the best thing is to leave him hanging."

Robert left me alone in the room and I looked down at the NDA agreement. I didn't look forward to the telephone call I had to make with Al Manchini. I could see my legal support for the King-Fu case flying out the window.

★ ★ ★

Sharlee showed up at one o'clock and we went into a small conference room and met with Ron Stevens and a manager responsible for purchasing, as well as one of their administration managers. With them we discussed pricing, the discount that Unipac was getting for doing the beta test, and the procedures Unipac preferred in dealing with suppliers. Sharlee thought of a number of important things, asked a lot of questions and she made it seem like she had been doing her job for a long time. I was glad she was there because my mind kept drifting to the telephone call I needed to make to Al Manchini.

After two hours of discussions we were finished and Ron Stevens said, "Would you like a tour of the factory?"

Sharlee nodded her head.

"Sure," I said. "That would be interesting." I had visited a few factories when I was doing my MBA, and his offer interested me.

Ron led us out of the building with the conference rooms and into an adjoining structure. It was a large building and Ron explained that three hundred people worked there. They were manufacturing a number of products including switches for Internet servers, and electronic pieces that would go into all sorts of wireless devices.

Machines were humming and assembly lines were moving parts

across them.

"Your TechZip system will help us get better control of all this inventory," Ron said. "It's a huge job to know what's out there and to keep track of it, but if your system works, then the savings for us could be significant."

The word was "if", I thought to myself.

We walked along and I was amazed at the speed and precision of some of the machines as they automatically soldered circuit boards and spun pieces around. People were checking machines and monitoring the flow of materials, as well as assembling things on production lines. They glanced at us when we walked by and I saw some men making their habitual eye movements at Sharlee.

When we finished with our tour we walked to the lobby. I took out my cell phone to order a taxi when I heard someone behind me say something to Sharlee.

"Well, hello Ms…"

"Sharlee Jackson," she said. "Hello Mr. Oliver."

I turned around and Sharlee was standing next to Sam Oliver, the founder and current Chairman of Unipac.

"Please call me Sam. It's all first name basis around here."

"And I go by Sharlee," she said.

He laughed. "It's a surprise to see you here."

"Unipac is going to be using our system so we came over to work out some details."

"Well, I didn't know that when we were talking yesterday. Looks like some of our people are one step ahead of me. That's good."

"Mr. Oliver, ah, Sam, may I introduce you to our CEO, Hank Morgan."

Sam Oliver shook my hand. His eyes penetrated like they looked into your soul.

"It's very nice to meet you," I said. This man was a living legend and I had difficulty to call him by his first name.

He said, "Yesterday Sharlee was telling me about your technology and it sounds quite interesting. You know that Unipac started as a packaging and inventory control company. We've diversified considerably, but still have operations that specialize in these areas."

I knew the story about Sam Oliver, how he had taken over a company started by his father and then expanded it. Besides being a great strategist, he was famous for good people management and fiscal discipline. "It must have been challenging to build your company,"

I said.

"Just make sure you work with the right people and everything eventually turns out right," he said. "Sharlee says your company is based in L.A. How many people do you have?"

"Ah…" How could I tell him that it was only two?

Sharlee interjected, "There are many of us when you count all the people from Campbell Labs."

"Robert Campbell?" Sam asked.

"Yes," Sharlee responded.

"That's impressive. Robert Campbell has saved our neck a number of times when we couldn't solve things. Of course I shouldn't admit our weaknesses to the outside world." He smiled. "And how long have you two been working together on this?"

What could I say, *two days*?

"We've been working together for thirteen years off and on," Sharlee chuckled.

"Thirteen years?" Sam looked puzzled.

"We went to the same Baptist church in central L.A. and have known each other since teenagers."

Sam Oliver laughed. "I like that. Long term business partners. By the way, my father was Baptist and I'm a chip off the old block. That's funny. It's not every day that these things pop up at the office, but I'm glad our paths crossed." He looked at me and said, "I'd like to know more about this system of yours. Do me a favor and keep me posted, but it's our business guys who will give the final go-ahead."

He shook my hand and then Sharlee's and he looked her in the eyes and said, "You know, you've made my day." And then he walked off down the corridor.

Sharlee turned to me and said, "He's a good guy."

"Yes he is," I said, thinking how Sharlee had been so quick on the uptake in answering his questions. She rescued me.

★ ★ ★

I kept putting it off until the end of the day, but finally got up some courage and called Al Manchini.

"Hello Al, this is Hank Morgan."

"Hank my friend, how's it going?"

"Okay. We had a busy day with the technology fair and all."

"So, how can I help you? You know I'm planning to come down to

L.A. on Monday and we should be able to package this pretty quick."

"Well, that's what I'm trying to call you for."

"We're still okay, right?"

"I'd like to postpone the due diligence," I said.

"Something else come up?"

"I'm not sure I need the funding."

"Are you talking with someone else?"

"Not really."

"You know that's a breach of good faith."

"I'm not talking with anyone else."

"Hank. You've got to understand that we've made an implicit pact to partner with each other in this."

"I understand, but I'm not ready."

"You sure? The funding and other services BMP Capital can provide will help you enormously."

"I need time to think."

"You know, last night you mentioned something about personal legal assistance. Even though you said it was a hypothetical question, I'm guessing, but somehow because of the way you said it I think it related to you. You know that we've got top-notch lawyers that can solve all your problems. Our guys move fast."

"My question was hypothetical," I said.

"Well, Hank, just think about it. When things heat up we can provide you with a lot of money and support... and, things will heat up." His voice sounded intimidating. "Just remember that we can take all your troubles away."

"That sounds good."

"So why not do it?"

I was tempted but remembered Robert's advice. "I want to consider my options."

"Well, you know now that your financing options are limited. You gave your word to deal only with us, an exclusive agreement. So, whatever you do, come to us before you talk with anyone else."

"Okay."

"What I'll do is call you Monday morning to see how we can progress."

"Okay."

We finished the call. It made me sick. I'm great when it comes to cracking people's heads, but when it comes to talking with people, sometimes an absolute wimp.

CHAPTER 24

Friday night we were tired and decided to fend for ourselves. I found a cheap taco restaurant close to the hotel, ordered four tacos and a soda, went back to my hotel room and watched an old movie. The tacos were like pieces of soggy cardboard filled with some kind of a greasy indeterminate filling. I couldn't really concentrate on the movie. The call with Al Manchini unsettled me. But there was also some good news. Sharlee had collected hundreds of business cards and she felt many of them would become serious leads. She seemed to be enjoying the experience and was getting much better at interacting with the attendees.

I was feeling positive about the success of my little company and knew we had to keep the momentum going. This was turning out to be a very strategic event for us and I was glad that Robert had suggested that we showcase TechZip here, if you could call it that.

All day Saturday we worked the booth together, Sharlee up front with the crowd and me in the background meeting individually with people. It was an exhausting day. At the end of it I invited her out to dinner and she accepted.

The fair ended at six o'clock so we went back to the hotel where I showered and put on clean clothing. On the rack the business suit still hung in its original flimsy plastic wrapping.

At seven-thirty Sharlee joined me in the lobby and we walked a couple of blocks until we found a fish restaurant. The place was hopping and we had to wait fifteen minutes before getting a table.

We ordered the meal and through much of it we talked about her studies and about Clyde and Rochelle. She updated me on what had happened to some of friends we had in our youth group at the Baptist church. There were some sad cases of some of them ending up on drugs or in prison, but I was surprised at how many of them had gone on to trade schools and universities. It gave me hope for an area of the city in which there is little hope.

While we were waiting for the check, I asked her how she liked being here.

"I'm having a great time," she said.

"You are?"

"Well, think about it. At the beginning of the week I was feeling like a reject, except for the care that Clyde and Rochelle were giving me. And all of a sudden I'm in San Jose meeting hundreds of people and having fun."

"But, it's not what you wanted to do," I stated.

"For sure, but sometimes you have to step through doors when they open."

"That's quite a door."

"You better believe it."

I glanced down at the table, paused and then looked at her. "I'm glad you're here."

"Really?"

"You give me confidence."

She smirked. "Come on. I give you confidence? I'm talking to Hank Morgan, the tough kid who was always ready to take on the world."

"Yeah, it may have looked like that, but the tough kid has some vulnerabilities."

"I understand. We both come out of a difficult world, but your experience was harder, I think."

"Maybe, but you never showed it, that things were hard," I said.

"Why is that?"

"You were always this cute kid, so happy and bubbly. I never thought about it until the other night when I saw you at Clyde and Rochelle's, but I looked forward to go to church because you were there."

She smiled. "Then I have to confess to you that I looked forward to seeing you there. I was heartbroken when you left for the Marines. Back then if I'd had a poster of you it would have been stuck up on the wall in my bedroom."

That made me laugh. "I liked you too, but you were a bit young… and there was the other thing, the community and all, with Jake and me being ah… in the minority."

"You mean the attitudes of people?"

"I guess." We both knew what we were talking about.

"Does it matter?" she asked.

"Does it?" I asked. I didn't know how to answer.

She said, "I think the fundamental principle is this; people are created in God's image. Because of that they have worth and dignity and that puts us all on a common platform. That's the starting point and the answers should flow from there."

"But the world doesn't see it that way. There are great walls of separation."

"Sure, but you didn't answer my question. Does it matter?" she asked.

"It shouldn't," I said, but knew that social barriers were sometimes more powerful than personal convictions.

"It doesn't mean anything to me," she said.

We didn't push it from there. It made me uncomfortable. A little sister I didn't want to hurt, but we looked at each other for a long moment, eyes locking and there was something much deeper. Her eyes were gorgeous.

I paid the bill and we walked back to the hotel and she slipped her hand inside my arm just above my elbow and I liked the way it felt. We took our time enjoying the warmth of the California night, moving effortlessly, like two rowers in a boat, gliding in tandem side to side.

Back at the hotel we went to the elevator and she got off at the second floor. Before leaving the elevator she kissed me on the cheek and said, "Thanks for the meal. You give me confidence too." And she turned and walked toward her room.

I went on to the third floor with the touch of her smooth lips burning against my skin.

CHAPTER 25

Sunday was another busy day at the technology fair. Robert was in meetings. Sharlee happily talked with people and was collecting business cards. She channeled quite a few people my way who represented large companies, the ones that showed serious interest in TechZip.

In the afternoon things were slowing and Sharlee moved to a chair next to a table and began sorting business cards, putting the serious leads into a separate pile. She joked that her legs had just given out. As far as I was concerned she had done a Herculean job.

Finally Robert began to fold up the tattered canvas Campbell Labs sign and then looked at me and moved a flat hand in a sword like movement across his neck, indicating it was time for me to close up shop. There was nothing to take back except the poster, so I began to roll it up. At the same time, I didn't expect to use that one again. I saw how the other companies had designed theirs.

As I took down my poster, Janie called my cell phone.

"Hank, I'm just checking in about seeing you tonight."

"Is it still okay?" I asked.

"Yes, I look forward to it. Still at eleven o'clock?"

"Sorry it can't be sooner. We're getting ready to head to the airport," I said.

"I'll be there. Did you get your money from the VC?"

"I decided to hold off."

"You what?" she asked.

"I've just decided to go cautiously."

"Well it's good to go cautious, but you will achieve your dream much faster if you have some money to work with."

"I know."

She paused. "Have you been listening to the black girl?"

"Her name is Sharlee."

"What did she tell you?"

"Nothing. I'm just concerned about the contract I signed with the VC. It's exclusive. It means I can only get financing from them."

Janie laughed. "That's all. Who cares where the money comes from? Why don't you just take the money and use it? You said they can help you with other things too."

I didn't remember telling her that. "They could get me a lawyer," I said.

"Why do you need a lawyer?"

"King-Fu is suing me."

"For the other night?"

"Yeah. Some high-powered lawyer is representing him."

"Then Hank, you need legal help."

"I know."

"And you said the VC can provide it."

"Yes, he said they could take my troubles away. In fact, he predicted that more troubles would come, that things will heat up, as though he sees through a crystal ball."

"I'm sure he has experience in working with entrepreneurs. Why don't you just accept his help."

"I don't know."

"Tonight we can talk about it," she said. "We can be alone, at your place."

"I'd like that," I said, the memory of caressing her curves coming forefront into my mind.

CHAPTER 26

Wwe got back to L.A. at nine o'clock and I drove Sharlee to her house. It was about a mile from Clyde and Rochelle's place. In the front of her house was a 'For Sale' sign stuck in the sparse grass yard. Overlaid on the front of the sign was a sticker that said, 'Sold'.

"When do you have to be out of here?" I asked.

"In two weeks. Do you want to come in?"

I looked at my watch. I did have some time before meeting Janie. "Sure," I said.

We went inside and the place was virtually empty. An old house always looks worse when there is no furniture. Here the walls were in much need of paint to cover a lifetime of spots and stains of two young girls growing up.

"My mother already moved all her things out and we got rid of some of the old furniture," she said.

There were just a few cardboard boxes in one corner of the living room. She led me into the kitchen where there were two plastic foldable chairs.

"Can I get you something to drink? Instant coffee, water? Why don't you take a seat?" She pointed to one of the plastic chairs while she moved to the other.

When I sat in the chair it felt like it would break. "Looks lonely here," I said.

"It is, but let's just say I'm not alone."

"Someone else is here?"

She smiled. "Spiritually speaking."

"You really believe it, don't you," I stated.

"I do. That's what'll get me through all this." She waved her hand around the empty room.

"There are a lot of memories here," I stated wanting to move on from that topic.

"My whole life was here. Now we're all moving on. I'm happy for my mother and sister."

"Things are going to work out for you," I said. That was the first positive thing I said in a long time. And I believed it. Anyone with her qualities would go a long way.

"They will," she declared. "For you too."

"Thanks. I hope they will. It looks like we are both facing some challenges."

"Our upbringing made us resilient. We can handle this," she said.

I liked the softness in her voice, yet there was assurance. "We'll get through it, at least you'll find a good place to stay."

"That's no problem. I can stay with Martine, but it would be nice to be on my own."

"With a job that pays you what you're worth."

She laughed. "My current job has some pretty good perks."

"Like what?"

"Business travel. Meeting billionaires. What else could you want?"

"Yeah, right. Look, I gotta go. Why don't you take off a couple of days? You worked hard on the weekend."

"Are you kidding me? I loved it. My legs are tired, but I want to be there tomorrow to work on all those leads, and we have quite a few action points from the Unipac meeting. I'll be at Campbell Labs at eight thirty."

She walked with me to the front door and I turned to her and said, "You're amazing."

"Come on, you know it's because I've got a great boss."

Her smile brightened my life. "I wish. You did a super job in San Jose. I was blown over by all that you did up there. Really, I don't deserve you."

"Sure you do."

She gave me a hug. I tried not to think about it, but I felt her shapely body against mine. It seemed to fit so nicely. I squeezed back and then we released.

"Thanks. See you tomorrow", I said.

★ ★ ★

The freeway traffic flowed well on the way back to Venice Beach and I go to my place at ten thirty, enough time to shower and put on clean clothes. I thought about my conversation with Sharlee and somehow I had the impression that she was way out of my league, in a much different way than Janie.

Sharlee had outdone me in San Jose by getting tons of leads and also her performance in the meeting with Unipac was outstanding. She even saved my neck when we met Sam Oliver, so cleverly answering his questions. And, it was incredible that he had even asked her to email him, two Baptists bonding together. All she did was far superior to my screw-up with Al Manchini and BMP Capital.

In fact, Sharlee was proactively taking on responsibility in TechZip without me even asking her. No, I didn't deserve her. I realized that she was exactly what I needed. Then I started to get concerned that I would lose her. She had applied for a number of jobs and any one of them might take her. What I was paying her was peanuts, just about all I could afford, but what would happen if she took one of those other jobs? I came to the conclusion that I would have to try my best to keep her with TechZip, but it seemed hopeless. Paying her a higher salary might help, but I needed the funding for that. Maybe I should just go ahead with the offer from BMP Capital? But here was my idiotic reasoning kicking in again and I resolved to make this company successful without them.

* * *

At eleven Janie hadn't arrived, and by eleven-fifteen I began to think she wouldn't come, but then I heard the deep rich Ferrari engine out in the parking area. I opened my front door just as she was getting out of the car. She was wearing shorts and a t-shirt and she came running up the steps and pushed me back into my apartment. A second later her t-shirt came off and there was nothing underneath.

She led me over to my bed and I lost track of time, a crazy blur that peaked, subsided and then started again.

Finally she lay back in my arms and I asked her, "What happened?"

"What happened where?"

"The other day, whenever it was, when the guy answered the phone and told me to get lost."

"That? Don't worry about it. Old boyfriend troubles. He just got a hold of my cell phone without me knowing it."

"And my car. He slashed a tire."

She laughed. "He did that?"

"Yes, outside your place in Malibu when it was parked up on Pacific Coast Highway."

"He's jealous. That's all. But, it's finished. He flew back to New York."

"But why the silence from you?" I asked.

She turned her head, her lips close to mine. "What do you expect? With him around am I supposed to be calling you all the time."

"But it's finished with him?"

"Of course. I just want you."

"The other day when Martha was here. What was that all about with you out in the car?"

"Nothing. I was coming by to see you. It just hurt me to see you with her, but Hank, let's now dwell on these things. The important thing is that we are together."

She moved her lips closer to mine and then moved back. "What about the money?" She said.

"The money?"

"Yes, the VC. You're going to take his money, aren't you?"

"I don't know."

"Hank, you're being stupid. The guy is going to give you money and help you with your problem with that terrible King-Fu. I shiver when I think how that drug lord placed his hand on me. You need a good lawyer to teach him a lesson. Can you do that for me?"

"Yeah." I hadn't thought of that and I hated drug dealers. The thought of King-Fu's hand on her and his wicked grin made me angry. I had fixed his grin, and beating him in court would feel even better, adding insult to injury.

"Then just sign the contract with the VC so that I can have some justice with King-Fu. Please."

Her lips touched mine and her hand dropped below my stomach.

"Ah, okay, I'll sign it."

Her lips parted and then the crazy blur started again.

CHAPTER 27

The following morning at eight o'clock Janie drove away. I wasn't sure I slept at all during the night, maybe some. She was like a tiger that wouldn't let me rest and I was exhausted.

I showered and shaved, got dressed and drove to a nearby donut shop where I ordered half a dozen sugar-glazed donuts and a black coffee. I ate all the donuts as I drove to Culver City and then sipped the coffee.

I arrived at Campbell Labs at nine-fifteen and when I saw Sharlee she said, "What happened to you?"

"Why's that?"

"Your eyes are red and you look… beat up."

I wanted to tell her that I went to the gym to work out, but I couldn't lie to her. "I had a rough night."

"I'll say."

"Couldn't sleep."

"Worries?" she asked.

"I guess." I tried to think of something to change the subject but my brain wasn't working. She did it for me.

"Robert said his guys finished the installation at Unipac on the weekend. The beta test is ready to start."

"Good. I guess I should go over there and start training people."

"Yes, like forty-five minutes ago."

"They're waiting for me?"

"Don't worry, Robert's already over there, but you better get going."

"Not too professional," I stated.

"No," she replied.

★ ★ ★

I drove fast and hoped there was no highway patrol around. The Unipac factory was in Inglewood. I was doing between seventy-five and eighty whenever I could get a free run, but most of the time the traffic slowed to fifty or less.

My cell phone rang and I answered it.

"Hello Mr. Morgan, this is Thomas Bennett from Bennett, Medici and Partners. Out of courtesy I just wanted to call you." His voice was slithery and sickening.

"What for?" I asked.

"My client, Mr. Horace Rice wants to move ahead with his claim for damages. I'm wondering if it's possible for me to meet with you and your lawyer to lay out our claims?"

"Tell King-Fu to stick it."

"Mr. Morgan I think you are being unreasonable. Is it possible for me to speak directly with your lawyer?"

"I don't have one."

"Mr. Morgan, I'm trying to be reasonable with you. My client's claims are significant and it would be prudent on your part to have some initial dialogue before this starts to escalate. I kindly advise you to obtain legal council."

"Okay, how do you want to play it?"

"I'll call you tomorrow and we will see when we can fix a meeting, the sooner the better."

"Then call me tomorrow."

I think Thomas Bennett had already hung up before I said that, but I couldn't tell because my attention got diverted to something different. Just behind me I saw a black and white car with a lights flashing. And then I heard the quick blast of a siren.

I worked my way over to the shoulder and the highway patrolman wrote me up for going ten miles an hour above the legal speed limit.

★ ★ ★

I slowed down the rest of the way and pulled into the large parking lot outside the Unipac factory. It was full and I could only find a free spot in a place that seemed about a mile from the building. Just as I turned off my engine my cell phone rang again.

"Hello Hank, this is Al Manchini. How's it going?"

"Al, it's not a good time. Can I call you back?"

"Sure, but this is just to let you know that I'm in L.A. and hope you have given this some consideration. We can help you. Are you ready to move forward?"

"I'm late for a meeting. Can I call you back?"

"I'll wait for your call my friend, but can you call me in the next couple of hours? We should meet today. I have to head back to the Bay area, so don't miss your opportunity."

"Okay," I said as I began running to the factory building knowing I was almost two hours late, as though that would make a difference.

CHAPTER 28

The rest of the morning was busy. Robert had switched things around a bit and for the first two hours of the morning he gave training to the people in the Information Technology Department on how to run the system. By the time I got there he had started the user training for twelve people who would be using the system. I joined right in.

We explained the different commands, how to pick up and assign new inventory coming into the system, and then all the virtual tracking features. They were amazed at how TechZip would simplify their lives and gain better control for Unipac. I could see that they were highly motivated.

When we broke for lunch I thought I would call Al Mancini, but something held me back. I felt stressed and wondered if I had a blood pressure problem. So many things were mounting up, including the tiredness I was feeling because of the lack of sleep last night. Being with Janie had shaken me to the core and my tiredness was more than physical. It was strange, but the only way I could describe it was like my soul had been separated from my body, feeling an unbelievable emptiness.

On the one hand I desired her more than anything I could imagine and when I was with her it seemed to release me from the emotional hang-ups I carried. I knew I carried some hidden aggressions that when triggered were extremely dangerous. I feared that I would kill someone, yet that's exactly what I wanted to do when I was in that state.

My aggressions were calmed when I had my fill of Janie. Yet this morning when we parted I felt an emptiness, even a funny kind of guilt where I couldn't identify the origin. It wasn't so much from the physical act of sleeping with her. That's everyday life where I grew up. There was something deeper, maybe like a betrayal, but I couldn't put my finger on it.

It wasn't that everything was perfect between us. It irritated me when she told me I was stupid for not accepting the offer from BMP Capital, like she was putting me down, questioning my business skills.

When I thought about BMP Capital there was something out of sync, but I couldn't put my finger on it. The 'exclusive' clause in the contract made me angry. Al's attitude was getting to me and I knew he was using pressure techniques used by salesmen by putting strict deadlines, like, the necessity to 'meet today', that he was 'on his way back to Silicon Valley' and that I shouldn't 'miss the opportunity'. That was pure manipulation. Why would he take such an interest in my project? There were thousands of opportunities for investment in the Bay Area.

One thing that kept coming back to my mind was Sharlee's words in San Jose, "I have my doubts, I have my doubts." And I offended her by negatively commenting on her lack of business knowledge. After all she had done up there, and her dedication of getting into the office this morning, it made me feel foolish. Her expression of doubt was restraining in a positive way. It's exactly what I needed, a sounding board to test ideas without running headlong into vain efforts.

If Sharlee knew I had been with Janie it would hurt her, maybe even devastate her. I was stupid to stay up all night like that and even though I had deeply desired Janie, that act clouded my ability to think straight today. It wore me down. And the fact is, it seemed like she was doing her best to keep me awake.

When I thought about it we hadn't really talked. I asked her a few questions, but she brushed them off. Of course she had other things on her mind and so did I, so it didn't seem to matter at the time, but now I wished I had gone into more detail on a few things. Exactly who is this lawyer boyfriend? Where does she stand with him? Why were there two guys in the car with her when she saw me with Martha? Why is she acting so mysterious?

All this was weighing on my decision with Al. The call this morning from Thomas Bennett raised my anger and I knew I needed legal help. BMP Capital could provide it. So, what was holding me back? I told Janie I would sign the contract, but in my mind I just couldn't hold the pen to sign my signature. What was wrong?

During our break in the afternoon my cell phone rang so I answered it. It was Al.

"Hank my friend, what's wrong?"

"Whats wrong?"

"Yeah, you were supposed to call me."

"Sorry, Al, but I'm busy."

"Still, it seems you're dragging your feet. In San Jose you seemed hot to trot and now it's something different. Remember that you gave your word and I took it in good faith, even made expenditures to come down here to L.A. I hope you remember the non-circumvention clause in the NDA?"

"I know. But, I didn't ask you to come to L.A."

"That isn't the way I perceived it. We were going to do due diligence and then you can have all the funding you need for your project."

That thought was appealing. "I just need time to think."

Al's voice lowered. "You're having troubles Hank, I can sense it. We are there to support you and will be beside you when things heat up. Remember that. Can we meet?"

"Not now," I said.

"Why?"

"I'm exhausted."

"What do you mean?"

"Just that, I'm exhausted and can't think straight. Can you call me tomorrow?"

"Okay, but we can't wait forever."

The phone clicked dead and I felt my head throbbing.

CHAPTER 29

I got home at eight o'clock, dog-tired, flopped on the bed and went immediately to sleep. Somewhere in the middle of the night I heard a knock on the door. I tried to open my eyes hearing a voice in the background.

"Hank, are you there?"

I got painfully got out of bed, lumbered to the door and opened it. It was Janie. She wore a long pink t-shirt with the word 'Nasty' on the front. The letters sparkled.

"What time is it?" I mumbled.

"Eleven, I always come at eleven."

"Janie I'm tired."

She put a hand on my chest and pushed me in and before I knew it the t-shirt was off. She wasn't wearing anything else.

"Oh no," I whimpered.

In a rush we were on my bed and she was pulled me to her and I entered a horrific zone of internal conflict between responding to my manly desires versus an overwhelming need to sleep.

Sometime in the middle of the night we stopped and she wanted to talk.

"Did you get the money?" She asked.

I wasn't sure what she said. "I need to… sleeeep." I dozed off.

She shook me. "No Hank. You can't do this to me."

I forced my eyelids open. "What?"

"I hate King-Fu. If you're any kind of a man you'll get legal help. I need justice. Do you love me Hank?"

"Uh huh." Coherent words were impossible.

"Then if you love me you will accept the assistance that the VC can offer. You promise to do that for me?"

"Uh huh."

"Tomorrow? You'll do it tomorrow?

"Uh huh."

"I love you Hank. Show me your love."

⋆ ⋆ ⋆

I felt done in and could hardly keep the Jeep on the road. It seemed like I was missing years of sleep and just wanted to pull off to the side of the freeway and shut my eyes for a few minutes. On the way to Unipac, Thomas Bennett called me again and I told him that I hadn't found a lawyer. He said he wanted to meet next Monday at nine o'clock in the morning at his office to discuss legal proceedings. That gave me six days to find a lawyer and prepare for the meeting. He gave me his address but I didn't write it down. I was having a hard enough time to keep my eyes on the road, let alone search for something to write with.

A few minutes later Al Manchini gave me a call and I told him I was still thinking about it. He put the sales pressure on me again only this time he got rude, even issuing a subtle threat, but then backed off and reaffirmed his offer for assistance when things heated up, as though things weren't hot enough already. Again, he said that BMP Capital could take away all my troubles. I told him I needed more time to think about it, we agreed that he would call me back tomorrow.

At Unipac the beta test was going well and it seemed that the users were operating the system without much help needed on my part. I wandered around and monitored how things were going, giving advice here and there and answering questions. Mostly I was just trying to make it through the day. A couple of times I went to the restroom and sat on the toilet, put my elbows on my knees, rested my chin in my hands and got a few minutes of sleep.

⋆ ⋆ ⋆

Once the workday was finished I stayed around to monitor a few of the control functions in the system to see that things were calculating properly. Everything seemed to be in order, so I went to my car and drove back to Venice Beach.

When I drove into the parking area next to my garage a sense of dread filled my soul. I needed to get a night of uninterrupted sleep, a break from Janie. This was worse than a nightmare, more like a torture chamber. She kept me awake all night and I wasn't able to think straight during the day. I was ready to agree to anything, to sign anything.

A number of times I wanted to call Al Manchini and say, "Okay, please take away all my troubles." There were a lot of questions spinning in my mind, but there was one thing that kept me from going ahead with Al. It was Sharlee's words that kept repeatedly ringing in my brain; "I have my doubts. I have my doubts. I have my doubts."

When I thought of Sharlee I felt guilty. I hadn't even called her today. Part of it was because I was busy, but that was just an excuse. At the bottom of it I felt I betrayed her. When I thought about it, she was one of the few people who were truly concerned about me, who wanted the best for me. And here I was getting stupidly carried away with a rich beauty queen.

Janie was a man's fantasy; wealthy, built like a centerfold, insatiable, everything I had ever desired. But now I questioned some things. It was like she was playing games with my mind, showing up at odd hours, controlling me, like a cat that plays with a mouse. Is this what I really wanted?

I walked up the steps to my apartment and the idea of her coming here became a living horror. I dreaded the thought of her unexpected knock on the door, and then keeping me awake all night, a worse fate than a Chinese water torture.

Beside that was her attitude towards things and people, like her insane emphasis on the material world, money-money-money, and putting down "that black girl and her simple clothing". It didn't fit with my view of the world, as screwed up as my view was.

What did I really want out of life?

I looked around my apartment. It was simple place, all that I could afford, but it had been functional for me for the past years. Granted, if I could make a descent living from TechZip, I would move into something nicer, at least where I didn't have to sleep in the living room, but I didn't need the grandeur of Janie's uncle's place at Paradise Cove. And that was only their West Coast home.

I went over to my bed and took my pillow and a blanket, stepped outside, locked the door behind me and went down to my Jeep. I drove a couple of miles, parked next to an abandoned warehouse, and got in the back seat. With my head against the pillow and blanket pulled over me, I went to sleep, safe from Janie's midnight torture chamber.

★ ★ ★

I woke and it was light and it took me a couple of moments to remember where I was. It was six forty five in the morning. I got out of the back seat of my car, stiff, but glad that I had an uninterrupted night of sleep. I drove back to my place to take a shower and get changed.

A couple of blocks away from my place I saw smoke in the air and when I got to my street there were three police cars at each end blocking it. Sticking out of the alley I saw a fire truck.

Quickly I parked my car and sprinted the half block to my place, but when I got there my garage and apartment were gone, as well as half of the wooden house. All I saw was a grotesque pile of smoking wood beams. A putrid smell filled the air.

Before I had time to think I heard someone say, "That's the crazy Marine over there; Urban-Rambo."

One of my neighbors, one of the mostly stoned characters that lived in the house was pointing at me. Next to him was a straight-faced man in a rumpled business suit. I couldn't tell if he was bald or if it was a short crew cut.

I walked over to them, stunned. "What happened?"

"Do you live here?" The man in the business suit asked.

"Well… yeah, but what happened?"

"And your name?"

"Hank, ah Henry Morgan."

"I'm Detective Grady from the L.A.P.D." He had a slow drawl when he spoke like he was from Texas or someplace down there.

"What happened?" I asked.

"Fire department received a call at three forty three last night. When they got here it was a full blaze, so all they could do was put it out and keep peripheral structures from catching fire. Where were you last night?"

"Ah…" I quickly thought. If I told them I slept in my car, they would become suspicious. "At a friend's house. We just talked late and I decided to spend the night."

"Who is your friend?"

"Jake Smith."

"And his address?"

I gave it to him, glancing over to what had once been a garage and house. There were large pools of black mud everywhere.

"Where we gonna live, man?" My neighbor asked.

Detective Grady ignored him and continued to look at me.

"How did it start?" I asked.

"No one knows except that your neighbor here says he saw movement last night and there was a light on in the garage."

"A light?"

My neighbor stepped between us and moved his face close to mine. "Yeah, there was a light on. I stepped outside for a smoke and saw the light and thought you were working."

"You're sure you weren't here last night?" Detective Grady asked me.

"No, well yes. I was here in the evening for just a few minutes but took off and didn't come back."

"What time was that?"

"Around eight or so, but only for a few minutes."

"Does anyone else have access to the premises?"

"No. Only me."

"And you weren't expecting visitors?"

"I rarely have visitors."

"Hum," he said.

"Where we gonna live, man?" My neighbor asked. His eyes were glazed. In spite of the rancid smoke from the ugly pile in front of us I thought I could smell of residue of pot on him.

"The fire department and our crime lab will have to make a thorough investigation as to the cause of this fire, knowing that there was a potential break-in last night. How can we contact you?" The detective asked.

I gave him my cell phone number.

"Do you have an address, a place to stay?"

"Sure, same place where I stayed last night." I gave him Jake's address and telephone number. "Can I look around?" I asked.

"Only from a distance and for now don't touch anything. We will also have to vacate the house, because of structural danger."

"I need to get my stuff out of there," my neighbor said.

"Sorry, but we can't allow you access," Detective Grady stated.

"That's not cool man."

"I suggest you contact your insurance company." Detective Grady had a slight grin.

"Yeah, right, man. That's not cool." My neighbor turned and walked away shaking his head.

I walked over to the edge of the smoldering wood and began to look through it as well as I could. The upper apartment had collapsed into the garage, but part of the garage was visible including the table where my computer had been. I couldn't see the computer. I went back to

Detective Grady. "May I ask you or your crime lab to look for a few things?"

"Like what?"

"My computer was on the table over there and I don't see it." I pointed into the rubble. "I also had important information in some of the binders. Maybe they can find them."

"Like what?"

"The computer and some of the binders held all of my detailed business plans. A couple of binders had other important information, like the record of my company registration and a patent application. There was also a lot of supporting technical details related to the patent. I'd just like to know if it's there."

His eyes shifted to my old jeep and then back to me. "You've got a patent? I'll make a record of that."

"What now?" I asked.

"We need to investigate. Someone will contact you." He reached into his coat pocket. "If you think of anything here's my number." He handed me a card.

I took it and looked at it: *Detective Curley Grady, Los Angeles Police Department, Arson,* and it included his cell phone number.

Detective Grady went over and talked with some of the firemen who were putting their equipment away. I stood there for a long time. My entire life was in that smoking rubble including the one and only photo of my mother holding me as a baby.

CHAPTER 30

I was devastated. If I could believe what my pot-head neighbor said, someone was in my garage and it looked like they had stolen things before lighting a match. Someone was turning up the pressure on me and I needed to take action.

I headed straight over to Wilshire Boulevard and to Sloppy Sam's Hamburger Heaven. Elena was wiping a table in the dining area and greeted me with a smile.. "Mr. Samouel is not here yet."

"Is Jake around?"

"In the kitchen."

I went into the back and found him looking at a recipe book.

He looked up. "Wow, you look like you've been to hell and back."

"I have," I stated.

"What's going on?"

"I need your help."

I told him about Janie's midnight visits and how that led to me sleeping in the car as the only way to get back some of my senses. And then I told him about the fire. I needed an alibi, a white lie.

He grinned. "I wish I could find a rich girl like that, but I know what it's like to have woman take you into the pit. In case anyone asks, you hung out at my place last night. And man, I'm sorry about your place. That hurts."

I said, "You know, when we first talked about Janie you said it was something like a rich girl who gets turned on by a bad boy kind of thing. Somehow I'm starting to think otherwise."

"How's that?"

"I don't know. It just feels like she's deliberately trying to pull me down."

"Another one we can add to the list," he stated. "By the way, I tracked Martha down."

"How'd you find her?"

"Through friends and their acquaintances. It took a while, but yesterday after work I went to see her. She was really upset to see me, complaining that I had ruined her life and a whole bunch of other accusations, but eventually she calmed down and then I asked her about visiting you. She thought I was jealous, so I just played that along and I said I was going to get even with you. Then I called her a loose woman."

"No kidding, Martha?"

"The one thing I learned during my short experience with her is how to get her excited, to question her integrity. So she got angry and denied that she was seeing you, and I pushed it and she confessed that she got paid to go visit you.'

"Paid?"

"Yeah, it sounds crazy, but two guys went to her place and gave her five hundred dollars to go see you. They also gave a bonus of another five hundred if she was seen kissing you outside your apartment. She was thrilled to have scored on that deal."

"You mean it was a setup?" I asked.

"It looks like it."

"Who did it?"

"She doesn't know. All she cared about was the color of the money.

Typical Martha."

"We pick some winners, don't we," I declared.

"You better believe it. What are you going to do now?

"I gotta find out what's going on. This is all too confusing."

"If you need help, let me know?"

"Thanks. Maybe I can sleep on your floor?"

"Anytime brother."

As I drove down Wiltshire Boulevard I remembered that I had told Janie about Martha the first time we met when we sat down at the hamburger joint in Malibu, when she bought me a glass of lemonade. I told her about the divorce with Jake and how Martha would do anything for money. Janie's reply was, "Really."

I needed to get to the bottom of this.

CHAPTER 31

I entered Campbell Labs and saw Robert over at his desk. He looked up when I came in. Sharlee was over in front of a computer concentrating on something. I walked over to Robert's area and sat down at his round table.

"I've got a problem and wonder if I could ask your help."

"What's up?" He asked.

I told him about my apartment and garage getting burned down and how it may have been on purpose, and that my computer and some company records may have been stolen. Then I updated him on all the pressure I was receiving from Al Manchini and Thomas Bennett.

Then it hit me. "Al Manchini had mentioned a number of times that things would heat up. I thought he was speaking figuratively, but do you think that's what he meant?"

Robert whistled. "This is weird stuff."

"I know. That's why I'm wondering if I could ask you for some special help."

"What's that?"

"I need to step away from the beta test at Unipac and spend some time to think about all this, maybe ask some questions to some people to see if there are any linkages. I'm wondering if you could manage the test to give me the free time to do some research?"

"For sure," he said without hesitation. Then he looked down at some electronic parts on his table, "but I've also got a deadline on this." He held up the part. "Look, I'll do what I can do."

I said, "Technical support is the most important, as the users seem to be operating the system by themselves. Although, it would be good to have someone onsite."

Robert looked across the room in the direction of Sharlee. "How about her?"

"I was thinking the same thing driving over here. If she could just stay over at Unipac until Friday, that would give me the time to do some research. I know she doesn't know much about operating the system, but at least that would give us a presence over there and she could escalate any problems to you."

"Let's propose it to her."

I went over to where Sharlee was sitting and tapped her on the shoulder. She turned and smiled at me. "Hank! Hi," she said.

Her voice triggered a rush of emotions, but mainly I felt I had let her down. "Hello Sharlee," I said. "I'm wondering if Robert and I could talk with you."

She had a look of concern.

"No, it's nothing bad. We just need your help and wonder if you could spend a few days over at Unipac."

"You want me to go to Unipac?"

"Yes. Just to give some presence onsite during the beta test, to show that we're not neglecting them."

"You're not going to be there?" She asked.

"No. Something happened. My apartment and garage burned down last night and I need to spend a few days taking care of some administrative things."

"Your place burned down?"

"Yes."

She was silent for a moment and then her eyes filled with worry. "I can't believe it. That's all you need… and I'm so sorry. This is terrible."

"That's what I'm thinking."

"Hank, is there anything I can do? Where will you stay?"

"With Jake."

"Look, if there is anything I can do for you, please let me know."

"If you go to Unipac that'll be a huge help. It frees me to do some other things."

"Whatever it takes," she said.

CHAPTER 32

I wasn't sure what I should be feeling, but the main sensation was numbness. I had lost my reference points. That apartment was all I knew for the past six years and now it was taken away. Outside of Clyde and Rochelle's, it was the one secure place in my life. Now it was gone. I realized that the only physical things I currently owned were the clothes on my back, an old Jeep, and a blanket and pillow in that Jeep. Sure there was some cash in the bank, but that wasn't really tangible. I guess I could include TechZip in my list.

I was sure that the initial shock of losing the apartment would wear off and then I would feel depression or anger, normal feelings within the grieving cycle. But it was too early for that. When I thought about it, my background in growing up had prepared me for this. As a child I would get moved to a foster home, get settled in, start to feel secure, and then they would move me on to someplace else. It should have been a constant cycle of shock and grief and anger, but when your entire life constantly gets taken away from you it becomes normal. You just learn to accept it and quickly adapt and move on to the new situation. But I carried a lot of anger; a fury that raised its ugly head when I least expected it. That scared me.

In spite of the fact that all my belongings had been burned up, I quickly rationalized everything and told myself that life is more than clothing and material possessions. I had friends who would stick with me through everything. Surely that was more important than how many things I owned.

Still, the loss of that place, one of my main reference points over the last years, was not easy.

But as I thought about it somehow things just weren't stacking up and I couldn't put the pieces of the puzzle together. When I thought about the fire I came to the conclusion that it wasn't an accident. During the six years I was there I never had any problems with fire. And the neighbor said he saw someone there in the middle of the night. Someone was out to get me, but who could it be?

Perhaps it was someone who didn't like me. Over the past week I had made some enemies starting with Jacko's gang members, and then King-Fu. I didn't think Jacko would do it. My encounter with him was amicable. He said I could walk his street anytime. Maybe one of his gang members did it, but if they did it without his blessing and

Jacko found out, it wouldn't go down well for them.

King-Fu was something different. He and three of his guys were still in the hospital. They might do something like this to get even, but a bullet in the head would be more like it. The question was, if he was in the process of taking me to court, why in the world would he burn my place? Would he endanger his case by doing something as stupid as burning down a building? And if he or any of his people did this, they certainly would not have gone into my garage. A little bit of gasoline and a match would have been sufficient.

There other loose ends, Al Manchini had kept using the term, "when things heat up." Was this related to the fire or was he just speaking hypothetically, knowing things at one time or another will get difficult for any startup company. I realized that I knew little about BMP Capital, even though I had signed an NDA with them. Maybe some due diligence was needed on my part?

And then there was Thomas Bennett, this high-powered lawyer. Why in the world would he lower himself to represent someone like King-Fu?

All of these things were unknowns and from this I started to devise a plan. First I needed to do some basic research and then I would determine which way to go from there.

★ ★ ★

After Sharlee left to go to Unipac I used her computer for a couple of hours to do esearch on the Internet. First I looked up BMP Capital. There wasn't much information available, although on their website they did have a list of "success stories" of companies they had funded. The companies were spread out all over the country, but most were in Silicon Valley. I printed out the list and began to look into some of the companies, making a note of who the company founders were. Perhaps some of those founders could provide some background information. Through a 'people search' website I found their addresses and I printed off maps and driving instructions.

Then I looked up the firm of Bennett, Medici and Associates. They had a one page website, more like a business card on the internet listing the addresses and telephone numbers of their offices in New York, San Francisco and Los Angeles. Somehow I needed to find out more about them. I printed that one page.

The Internet research didn't take me far, but at least it gave me something to go on. There was one other item of doubt in my mind and that was Janie's strange behavior. When I thought about it, I didn't know that much about her, other than the fact that her family had a house in Malibu, and another back east somewhere, that she was a history or pre-law student at Vassar, and she drove a Ferrari. She also had an extensive wardrobe that came out of fashion magazines. There was also the fact that she misled me on our first two dates. She said she was going home to Malibu, yet I followed her to a house in Beverly Hills where she had access to an automated gate.

I went to the Vassar University website to see if there was a list of students, to see if I could find a Janie Carlton, or Jane Carlton. The school did not list their students. Somehow I needed to find out more about her.

I needed some help to do this and looked around the room and saw Freddy, Robert's communications guy. He looked like the type who could do some market research for me. I went over to his desk and asked him if he would do a favor to try and find some information. He agreed to do it.

In one corner of the room on some shelves Robert had a pile of canvas shoulder bags, 'giveaways', with Campbell Labs printed on one side. I put my printouts into the canvas bag and walked out to my Jeep.

I drove east on I-10 to West Los Angeles. I kept within the speed limit, not needing to get another speeding ticket. As I drove along I noticed a dark car that was behind me traveling at the same speed me and always maintaining the same distance. I became concerned.

There was an off ramp up ahead and I quickly decided to make like I was going to take it and pulled over into the far right lane. The dark car did the same. I put on the right hand turn signal and started to turn onto the off ramp, but in the last possible moment swerved back onto the freeway. I saw that the driver in the dark car behind me was confused. He was getting ready to take the off ramp and then he swung back onto the freeway. He took up the same speed and distance as before.

Now I was certain I was being followed.

My Jeep was old and just about any car any car in the world could easily outrun me, so I just stayed with the flow of the traffic and began to work my way into the far left lane. The car following me did the same. Then I waited until the next off ramp and at the last possible moment I swerved to the right across lanes. Some cars hit their brakes and horns were honking, but I made to the off ramp.

The dark car was blocked by other cars, so was forced to keep going straight on the freeway. I tried to see who was in it and it seemed there was two people in the car, but the windows were dark tinted and things were happening so fast that I couldn't really get a good view.

As I pulled off the off the ramp onto a major street, I realized that my hands were shaking.

CHAPTER 33

It took me a while to find him. I started with Mama Caterina who gave me a lead to someone, who told me to go to a Mexican Bar just off Lorena Street.

I walked in and it took a moment for my eyes to adjust to the darkness. There was a lively Mexican mariachi song playing from loudspeakers, and fifteen or twenty Hispanics were in the place, mainly drinking beer. The smoke was thick. They tended to smoke brands from their home countries, the equivalent of smoking coal tar.

I saw him seated at a corner table. Several of his gang members were at the table with him. One, a thick-necked guy with tattoos, had bandages across his nose. When the guy with the bandaged nose saw me his eyes turned wide.

I walked up to the table and Jacko smiled. "Morgan, *amigo*, strange place to see you."

"It took me a while to find you."

"You look for me?"

"I wonder if we could talk?"

"Talk is free." He laughed. "Bring a chair."

"Could we talk alone?"

His eyes scanned the three guys at the table and he waved the back of his hand in a wide sweeping movement across the table. "Go!"

They got up and went to the bar and he moved an open hand in the direction of one of the empty chairs. "*Por Favor,*" he said.

We talked for thirty minutes and in the end he agreed to do a few things for me. It cost me some money but I knew that Jacko would know how to get it done. I told him I would be gone for a couple of days, but gave him my cell phone number. He said he would call me on the weekend.

Three hours later I was on a flight to San Jose.

CHAPTER 34

In my research on the Internet I had found a car rental company near the San Jose Airport that was less than half the price of the main car rental agencies. The agency picked me up in a dusty old van and drove fifteen minutes to an area with rundown companies and then into a dark unlit sales lot for used cars. Most looked like a bunch of wrecks.

The guy who picked me up handled the paperwork and he said, "Just pick one out, whatever you want." I did my best, but it was night and difficult to see.

After checking out the car I drove south of San Jose on El Camino Real and then off on a side street to the cheapest motel I could find, a set of old wooden bungalows.

On the flight to San Jose I calculated my cash position. Because of having to pay Sharlee a salary, and what I was going to pay Jacko, I had about two weeks of cash left in my bank account. After that I would probably have to drop everything and go find a real job. I was attempting to hold my expenses to a bare minimum.

In the motel room I couldn't tell if the sheets had been washed of not, being full of different shades of yellow and brown stains. Because of the lack of sleep over the previous nights I put my head on the pillow and slept like a rock.

I got up at five o'clock in the morning, took a shower, and put on the same clothing I'd been wearing for two days, picked up the canvas bag with the printouts and left the room. After settling the bill, I went to my rental car and for the first time saw it in the daylight. It was an old Chevrolet covered with rust and dents.

It took several tries before the car started. It sounded like it needed a tune-up. At least the price was within my budget. Then I headed north on Highway 101. The traffic was bumper-to-bumper, people going to work.

My first destination was Mountain View. There were four people on my list taken from the BMP Capital website. I picked them because of their relatively close proximity to each other. I felt it would be possible to visit all of them in a day or two. Other people on the BMP Capital list were scattered across the country; Seattle, Portland, Chicago, Boston and other major cities. It would be impossible for me to visit them all. I had thought about giving them calls before meeting with them, but decided against it. I didn't want to alert the wrong person.

The slow traffic gave me time to think, but I hoped that it wouldn't make me late to meet the first person on my list.

In driving north I thought about the San Francisco Bay Area and how so many companies had started in this area. For years it had been a place of innovation and in the 'dot.com' days it was a hotbed of new company formation. Technology was bursting at the seams and everyone was trying to start a company. Since the burst of the dot.com bubble the number of new startups had slowed down somewhat, but Silicon Valley was still one of the leading places in the nation for creating new technology companies. Because of that I understood why so many venture capital companies were based here, including BMP Capital.

After leaving 101 I headed into Mountain View. Just like the cities in Los Angeles, it is difficult to know where one city ends and the other begins. I was working off the map and driving directions I pulled off the Internet.

The address I was looking for was a private residence, as that was all I had to go on. The map led me to a small house in a residential area. The clock on the dashboard of the car was the only thing that was working. It said six-thirty. The gas gauge said empty, but the guy at the rental agency said the gauge didn't work and that the car was full.

There was a light on in the house, so I walked up to the front door and knocked. A man about thirty-five opened the door. He was wearing a t-shirt and dark pants. His hair was wet, so I assumed he had just showered and was getting ready for work.

"Excuse me, but are you Mr. Watford, Peter Watford?" I asked.

"Yes, what's going on?"

"I'm sorry to bother you so early in the morning, but I didn't know how else to contact you. My name is Hank Morgan. May I ask you a question?"

"You trying to sell something?"

"No, not at all. I'm an entrepreneur and would like to ask your advice about something. I flew up from L.A. to see you."

"From L.A.?"

"It's important."

"Look, I don't have much time. Need to get to work."

"Please, could I just ask one question? It shouldn't take long."

"What's the question?"

"On a website it said you were the founder of a company called Voice-Link. It looks like BMP Capital was the VC firm behind your company. What can you tell me about them?" What I had read on the BMP Capital website was that Voice-Link had been sold to a telecommunications company for three hundred million dollars.

"BMP Capital?"

"Yes," I replied.

"I can tell you this." His lips tightened. "They can go to hell."

I was surprised. "Why do you say that?"

"Why do you want to know?" He asked.

"Because they have contacted me and I want to check them out before going any further."

"Did you sign an Non Disclosure Agreement with them?"

"Yes."

"Bad news. If you want, come on in for a quick coffee while I get dressed."

"Thanks." Coffee sounded good.

Peter Watford led me through a small living room and then into a dining room connected to an open kitchen. He got a coffee cup from a cupboard and poured me a cup of fresh brewed coffee. I sat down on a tall stool next to the kitchen counter.

"Just a minute," he said as he left through a hallway.

I looked around. The living room, dining room and kitchen were small. It was an older house, but appeared to have gone through a renovation. The hardwood floors and kitchen seemed new. At the same time, I wondered if this fit someone who had been the founder of a company that was sold for three hundred million dollars?

Peter Watford came back and was buttoning his shirt. "Don't mess with those guys." He poured himself a coffee and then sat down on a stool on the opposite side of the counter from me.

"Why do you say that?" I asked.

He sipped his coffee and looked me in the eye. "Tell me a little more about yourself."

"As I said, my name is Hank Morgan and I have a startup company based in L.A. Besides that I'm a graduate of UCLA with an MBA."

"Do you have a business card?" He asked.

I pulled a card out my wallet and handed it to him. I only had a few left, as the rest were burned in the fire.

He looked at it and said, "Okay." He put it on the counter. "Don't trust those guys."

"Why? What was your experience with them?"

"A living nightmare. I had grown my company and needed an

injection of capital and they came on all sugar-and-sweet, and I got carried away. Signed an NDA and then a full-blown venture capital contract. Then everything went bad. One of the clauses in the contract was that if I missed a milestone they had the right to bring in new management. I was optimistic and agreed to the terms and conditions, and then missed a milestone. They pushed me to the side."

"But, your company was sold for a significant sum of money. Surely you participated in that?"

"Are you kidding me? Once they had control they could do anything they wanted through all kinds of accounting tricks. I ended up with very little, enough to fix up my house and that's about it."

"Couldn't you take legal action?"

"I tried, but they just had too much power and the contract was solidly in their favor."

"When you say they were all sugar-and-sweet, how was that?"

"From the first day I met those guys they seemed to know my needs. In fact, as I began to work with them I had the impression they knew more about me than I knew about myself. Therefore they knew how to pull my strings."

"How did they know so much about you?"

"Who knows? I guess they just did their research. In any case they stole my company and there was nothing I could do about it."

He finished his coffee. "Look, I've got to run. My only advice is to stay away from them." He took our cups to the sink, rinsed them and put them in the dishwasher. "If you need any more information please give me a call."

"Thank you," I said. "Could we also keep our discussions discrete?"

He mockingly laughed. "I'll never talk to BMP Capital again as long as I live. Are you sure you signed a Non Disclosure Agreement with them?"

"Yes," I answered.

"Bad news."

CHAPTER 35

The car sputtered when pushed above fifty-five. I drove north on 101 past Palo Alto and exited at Redwood City. The next address I had was for an entrepreneur named Robert Montet. The driving instructions took me into a residential area that looked similar to that of Peter Watford, small homes with tall fully-grown trees.

I found the address I was looking for but it was eight o'clock and I thought it would be too late to meet with him. At least I could try.

I parked the car, walked up to the front door and knocked. There was a peephole in the door and from the other side I heard a woman's voice yell out, "What do you want?"

"Is it possible to speak with Robert Montet?" I asked.

There was silence on the other side. I stood there and waited. Finally the door opened slightly, wide enough to be held by a safety chain.

A woman's face appeared. "What do you have to do with Robert?" She asked.

"I'd just like to ask him a few questions if possible."

"Are you from the police?"

"No ma'm. I'd just like to seek his advice."

"He's not here anymore." She had gray hair and I guessed she was somewhere around sixty or sixty-five years old.

"Do you know where I can find him?"

She hesitated. "He passed away. I'm his mother."

I saw sadness on her face. "I'm very sorry to hear that… and I'm sorry if I bothered you."

She looked up at me. "What do you want to know?"

"Well, I was hoping to ask him a few questions."

"You didn't know Robert?" She asked.

"No, I didn't, just that he had his own company and I'd like to find out some things about that."

"Like what?" She asked.

"About a venture capital firm he used called BMP Capital."

Her eyes narrowed. She hesitated and then reached up and released the safety chain and opened the door. "Come in."

We went to the living room and I sat in a large comfortable sofa-chair and she sat on the couch off to my right. She was a small woman with narrow wrists.

"What can you tell me?" I asked.

Her eyes looked down to her hands folded in her lap. Her right thumb began to move back and forth over the top of her left hand. "He was a good boy," she said, "although he rarely told me what he was doing with his company. It was some kind of technology, very advanced he said. I didn't understand. It took him a lot of hard work to build it up and he started to sell some products. And then something went bad. He wouldn't tell me."

"You have no idea what it was?" I asked.

"Not really, other than he was running out of money and like so many of these startup companies you read about in the paper, there was always talk of venture capital. He told me that the inflow of money from venture capitalist would solve all his problems."

"Did he work with BMP Capital?"

"Yes, he did and then something went wrong, but he didn't tell me. It got to a point where he was angry, where he got a lawyer to sue BMP Capital, but he also got very nervous, jumping every time the telephone rang."

"And may I ask how he died?"

"He… supposedly… jumped off the Golden Gate Bridge." Her eyes filled with tears.

"I'm sorry to hear that."

She looked up. "It wasn't like him. He was always a brave boy and that was so not like him."

I didn't know what to say. If someone is pushed to the limit they can do irrational things. "Do you have any idea why it happened, why it went so far?"

"No, as I said he was under business pressure."

"And what happened to his company?"

"Oh, after he died the company just folded. BMP Capital managed all of that."

"And he, or you got nothing out of it?"

"BMP Capital had invested in Robert's company. They were able to sell some of the assets; some patents I think and I guess there were some other things. Then the creditors were paid off and the shareholders received the rest."

"And that was you?"

"Robert had a will. Half went to me and half to Carole, his fiancée, Carole Gunnerson. They would have been married by now. We each received half a million dollars. I'd rather have Robert than the money."

I absolutely understood how she felt but didn't know how to respond other than, "Losing a loved one is not easy." But behind it somehow the distribution of money didn't make sense to me. The BMP Capital website said that the company had been sold for fifty million dollars. I wondered who got the rest?

We stayed quiet for a moment and then I asked, "You mentioned his fiancée. Would she know anything?"

"Probably more than me. She's not technical, but she discussed company things with Robert."

"Do you think I could talk with her?"

"I suppose. We don't stay in touch so much, you know, as time passes by. But I can give you her phone number. She works during the day."

"That would be helpful," I said and then I thought of something. "One other thing. Would you happen to have the original contracts that Robert signed with BMP Capital or know where I could find them?"

"Just a minute." She got up off the couch and went into a room down the hall. In a couple of minutes she came back with a binder. One the side there was handwriting that said, 'Contracts'. "Maybe in here," she said. "I retrieved this binder out of his office after he died."

I took the binder and flipped through it. There were a number of contracts with suppliers, outsourcing contractors, and a few employees. There were two contracts with BMP Capital, the NDA and the contract with the venture capital terms and conditions.

"May I make photocopies of these?" I asked. "I could get it back to you in an hour."

"Sure, go ahead and take your time."

"And can you give me the name and telephone number of Robert's fiancé?

She gave me Carole Gunnerson's telephone number and I went to my car and set off looking for a photocopy shop. There was one about a half a mile away. In thirty minutes I had the originals back to her.

I drove away from her house and pulled into the parking lot of a strip-mall and looked at the contracts. The NDA was exactly like mine, a simple one-page agreement containing the same exclusivity clause. The venture capital contract was another matter, with pages and pages of legal jargon that would be unintelligible to the average entrepreneur.

I flipped through it reading phrases here and there until I came to the end and saw the signatures and then wondered if something might be wrong. I looked at the signature on the NDA. On both contracts the signatures seemed to be exactly the same, the same length and size. I overlaid one signature against the other. They were on the same place on the signature line. Either Robert Montet was a perfectionist or something was amiss. What are the probabilities that two signatures would line up like that? Of course I wasn't knowledgeable of these things and the question was how could I find a handwriting expert?

⋆ ⋆ ⋆

I realized that I had turned off my cell phone when I boarded the airplane in Los Angeles and had forgotten to turn it back on. I had five messages. Before going to them I first tried to call Carole Gunnerson but there wasn't an answer. I didn't leave a message.

Then I went back to the five messages in my com-box. Three were from Al Manchini asking were I was and with him ranting on, "we gotta talk." One was from Robert Campbell that had been registered about an hour ago and the other from Detective Grady. Both asked to call them back.

I called Robert first.

"Hello Hank," he said. "We've got a problem at Unipac."

"What's happening?"

"Something in our system is double counting the inventory, or at least some selected items. I'm not sure what it is."

I thought through the software logic and everything we had tested in the lab had worked fine. "Are the selected items random, or are they of a certain type?" I asked.

"It looks like it's random."

That scared me. It could mean delaying the beta test until we could fix the problem, which might take a long time and by that point I would be out of cash.

"What's our course of action?" I asked.

"Sharlee's working on it. I'll head over there in an hour once I finish a critical job here in Culver City."

"Sharlee? She doesn't know anything about the software."

"Give her credit," he said. "She can at least help pacify things over there."

"Okay, let's do our best," I said, knowing we didn't need a pacifier over at Unipac, but rather someone who could fix the problem.

He said. "Don't worry. I just wanted you to know. Now, tell me, how things are going up there?"

I gave him a brief update on my two meetings with Peter Watford and Mrs. Montet. We hung up and I called Detective Grady.

"Grady here," he said.

"Detective Grady, this is Hank Morgan. You tried to call me."

"Yeah. You wondered about the computer. Our crime lab guys didn't find it."

"You're sure?"

"They looked through everything. It wasn't there. They also looked for the binders you asked for. As you saw, the place was significantly damaged, but our guys are experts at uncovering evidence. They didn't find the binders."

"Do you think someone stole them?"

"Well, it looks like there was someone in your garage the night of the fire and the crime lab found evidence that someone started the fire."

"Like how?" I asked.

"We'd prefer to keep that confidential until the investigation is finished, or at least for now."

"I understand," I said. "Is there anything I can do?"

"Not really," he said.

Then I had an idea. "Do you have any handwriting experts at your police department."

"For sure. Why do you ask?"

"I wonder if you have someone who could compare two signatures?"

"Does it relate to the current investigation?"

"I don't know, but it might."

"Then why don't you bring it over."

"I can't because I'm calling from Silicon Valley."

"What are you doing up there?"

"Just some research for my company, but I'll be back in L.A. on the weekend. Could I bring it in then?"

"I'm off on the weekend."

"How about tomorrow afternoon? I can try to catch an earlier flight."

"Okay, just let me know."

"I will," I said, wondering if I was doing the right thing by getting him involved.

CHAPTER 36

I drove further north on U.S. Route 101 and then followed the preprinted maps to the homes of the next two people on my list. They lived exactly five miles away from each other, according to the specificity of the driving instructions printed off the Internet. No one was home at the first place. At the second I introduced myself to a woman who answered the door and told her I was looking for a James Robinson. It was his wife. She called to his workplace and we arranged a meeting at his home at five-thirty.

It was two o'clock in the afternoon and I knew I had a few hours to kill, so I found a large shopping center and went in and bought a shirt in a discount department store and in a drugstore bought a razor, toothbrush and deodorant. The shopping center had a food court, so I took a Chinese meal, my first food of the day.

It wasn't even close to the same quality of Chinese food that Janie had brought the first night she came to my apartment. I didn't want my mind to go there, because it was painful to think of the games she had been playing with me, "the bad boy toy to be used, get tired of, and just throw away," as Jake had claimed.

From the canvas shoulder bag I took out the printout of the list of companies from the BMP Capital website. There were thirty-two companies listed. Twelve of them had 'in progress' next to the company. The remaining companies on the list had been sold and the sale price of each company was listed next to it.The buyers were mostly large well known multinational companies operating in various sectors of the electronics industry. I was relieved to see that Unipac was not on the list. The lowest sale was thirty five million dollars and the highest was six hundred million.

What surprised me was that there were no Initial Public Offerings of any of the companies that BMP Capital had funded. In other words, no company had stayed an independent stand-alone company, either privately held or publicly traded on the stock market. It just seemed strange to me that all the companies had been sold to other buyers and not one of them went IPO.

I added up the sale prices of the twenty companies and the total came to just over four billion dollars with an average of close to two hundred million per sale. That meant that the twelve 'in progress' companies added another two billion dollars into the equation.

I was dumbfounded. Based on the two examples from this morning, very little of the revenue from the sales had gone to the founders of the companies. That meant that most of the revenue from the sale was going into BMP Capital. Was it the same with these other companies? Were they running some kind of a scam?

In fact, I understood how easy it would be to take advantage of new entrepreneurs, like me. But, many of the founders of these startups were experienced managers who should have been aware of the dangers of going with a venture capitalist. What caused them to get involved with BMP Capital?

As I thought about this I began to doubt myself. Were my assumptions merely fantasy? They had to be. But I was getting concerned. To what end would they go to steal the founder's companies? Did they drive people to suicide? Would they burn my apartment to achieve their objectives? My mind was running away.

My cell phone rang and it was a number I didn't know and I hesitated on whether to answer it.

"Hank Morgan," I answered.

"Hank, it's me." It was Sharlee. "It sounds noisy wherever you're at?"

"I'm in a food court in a shopping center in Silicon Valley."

"Eating upscale," she laughed.

Her voice warmed me. "Just glad to be eating," I said.

"Robert Campbell told me that you were up there to do some research. I'm just calling you to let you know that the beta test is back on track."

"That's good news. Did Robert fix it?"

"Robert? No. He didn't need to come. I worked with the people here at Unipac and we figured out what the problem was. They weren't using the system right, but there is also a weakness in our system. We can improve it if we just build in some simple safeguards."

I said, "Sharlee, you're a dream." I couldn't believe that she fixed it. I felt like an idiot for my thoughts about her, about not needing a 'pacifier' over at Unipac.

"Thanks Hank." She paused. "I'm really sorry about your apartment. Again, if there is anything I can do just let me know."

"I appreciate that." What good would that do, but honestly I welcomed that gesture.

"Do you think it was arson?"

"That's what I'm going on."

"It's absolutely scandalous. I hope you can find them and they get their justice."

"I'm just trying out some leads."

"You know this really angers me… to see this happen to you."

"Thanks Sharlee."

"Just be brave, and could you promise me that you'll let the police take care of it if you find out who did it?"

"You mean you don't want me acting like I normally do?"

"Hank, you know what I mean. I don't want you to get hurt."

"I'll try."

"When are you coming back?"

"Hopefully tomorrow."

"That's good. Will you be coming by Unipac?"

"I'll probably get in too late and then I've got to follow-up on a few things on the weekend."

"Okay, see you on Monday," she said.

"Sharlee, thanks for your support."

We hung up and I thought, one tough lady, so much like Rochelle.

CHAPTER 37

At five-thirty I drove to the home of the third entrepreneur on my list named James Robinson. He was a computer engineer with an MBA from Stanford and had twenty years experience in working in technology companies.

I introduced myself and reiterated what his wife had told him on the telephone, that I was an entrepreneur seeking advice on BMP Capital.

He led me into a den and his wife brought some fruit juice. She closed the door as she left, leaving us alone to talk.

"What would be your advice concerning BMP Capital?" I asked.

"Run for cover," he said.

"Why do you say that?" I asked.

He told me his story that was very similar to that of Peter Watford, the first entrepreneur I met this morning. BMP Capital had come across very professional, he partnered with them, and then they drove him out of his company.

When he was finished I said, "Everyone else I have met with has given me the same message, to stay away from BMP Capital, yet somehow they manage to keep signing contracts with new companies. It's seems they'd be developing a bad reputation by now."

"They manage their reputation very carefully," he said. "They have a very strong marketing and sales team, and are backed up by some lawyers that know how to play hardball. If there's anything bad said about them, they will go after you. And they're good at intimidating people. Believe me, I know."

"But, what you're telling me about them now is entirely negative."

"I'd never say anything in public. My wife and I are just getting on with our lives."

"Your wife and you?"

"That was part of what went wrong. Our marriage almost broke apart, but now we've got a good relationship and we want to keep it that way. BMP Capital would make things uncomfortable for us."

I was confused. Why was he talking about the relationship with his wife? "I don't mean to get personal, but how does this fit with BMP Capital?"

"I'm embarrassed to say it, but I found out that BMP Capital set me up after it was way too late."

"How's that?"

"A year and a half ago I met a woman. She was a real knockout and it quickly led to an affair. She seduced me. Someone took photos and then I was blackmailed. That was happening at the same time I was starting discussions with BMP Capital, and they introduced the idea that they would help me in any way, in order to make me successful. I was meeting with someone named Al Manchini."

I nodded.

"You know him?" he asked.

"He's the one who is putting pressure on me."

"Be careful. He's a snake. In my case I cracked and told Al Manchini my blackmail problem and he laughed and said they would take care of it. He said their lawyers were connected to world-class private detectives and they could find the blackmailers. I was desperate and signed the contract then and there, and because of it I lost my company."

"And you think BMP Capital was behind the blackmail?"

"For sure. It was only afterwards when I started to think straight again. There were things I confided with this woman, and then later Al Manchini was playing them back to me. I'd stake my life that they were behind it."

"Your wife knows?" I asked.

"She's a champion. It was tough for a while, but she stuck by me."

"May I ask what the woman looked like?"

"Tall, blond, brown eyes, small scar under her left eyebrow. Do you want more graphic details?"

"No thanks." It wasn't Janie. I slumped back in my chair.

He must have seen my relief because he smiled. "Same thing with you?"

"I don't know. I'm still piecing the whole thing together. That's why

I'm doing this research."

"Are you married?"

"No," I answered.

"Doesn't matter. These guys will find a way to get to you. Like I say, they play hardball and will do anything to win."

"Thanks for the advice."

"I never met with you," he said.

"You're that frightened of them?" I asked.

"You better believe it."

CHAPTER 38

I drove the five miles over to the house of the fourth person on my list. I probably should have called ahead to make an appointment, but meeting with James Robinson gave me this uneasy impression that I shouldn't be announcing myself too much. I didn't want BMP Capital to get wind of my investigations.

I waited until eight thirty, but no one ever came. Then I remembered that I had to call Carole Gunnerson, the fiancée of Robert Montet. After the first ring she answered her phone.

"This is Carole Gunnerson," she said.

"Ms. Gunnerson, my name is Hank Morgan. I'm wondering if it is possible to ask you a few questions?"

"I know," she replied. "Mrs. Montet called me. I'm willing to meet with you."

"Thank you," I said. "Are you able to meet now?"

"No, this isn't a good time. I'd suggest tomorrow at noon."

"Do you know of a restaurant or a place to meet?"

"I'd rather be discrete. You know the way to Mrs. Montet's house. She said we could meet there."

"I'll be there at noon," I said.

★ ★ ★

I had trouble starting the car and was worried that I would completely drain the battery, but it eventually started and I made my way to highway 101 and drove south back to Redwood City. I found a cheap hotel slightly better than the motel where I stayed last night, except that the television didn't work. I didn't care. I was tired. I turned off my cell phone not wanting to be bothered, especially by Al Manchini or Thomas Bennett.

It felt good to take a shower and shave. I dressed and walked down the street to a greasy spoon restaurant that had some kind of special on hotdogs. I bought three and went back to my room and devoured them in about a minute.

I got my new toothbrush out of its wrapping and used it, the first time I had brushed my teeth in two days, and sensed how something as simple as that could be so satisfying. At least I could now add a toothbrush to my list of worldly possessions.

I got in bed and thought about Sharlee and how much she resembles Rochelle. Tough love. And then I was out.

The following morning I woke up at nine and realized that I had slept eleven hours. The reading light was still on next to my bed. I called the airline and rebooked for an earlier flight. calculating that I would have one hour with Carole Gunnerson. Then it would take half an hour to get to the airport. There was a two fifty flight available. That would get me into L.A. in time to meet with Detective Grady.

After rebooking the flight I had some time to kill, so I took the printouts from the canvas bag and began making notes on the back of them, trying to recall as much information as I could from the interviews and seeing if there were any angles I had missed. All I could make out was that BMP Capital was a dangerous company to be dealing with.

Then I showered and shaved, and put on my new shirt. It felt good to be wearing something clean, although it was strange to know I only had two shirts to my name.

I turned on my cell phone and saw that Janie had tried to call me three times. I was tempted to call her, but decided against it. Even though she had been playing with my head, my body longed for her. It scared me to think that I might have some kind of addiction for her.

There was also a message from Al Manchini. "Hank, I need to urgently talk with you. In trying to track you down I learned about your burned apartment. I'm telling you that we can help you with things like that. For entrepreneurs things will go wrong, and we are there to help when things heat up… and they will."

I listened to it again, and after what James Robinson, had told me yesterday, I definitely interpreted it as a threat. But what could they do now? Take something? The only thing I owned was an old Jeep and a couple of shirts.

At eleven forty-five I checked out of the hotel and drove over to Mrs. Montet's house. A red Corvette was stationed where I had parked the Chevrolet yesterday. I pulled in behind it, went up to the house and knocked on the door. I heard the safety chain come loose and the door opened.

Mrs. Montet stuck her head out, looked up and down the street and then motioned for me to come in. She led me to the living room and introduced me to Carole Gunnerson. She got up from couch and shook my hand. She was about five foot four, just a bit taller than Mrs. Montet.

I sat down in the same sofa-chair as yesterday and Mrs. Montet left the room. There was a plate full of homemade chocolate chip cookies on the coffee table. My stomach growled.

Before I could say anything Carole Gunnerson said, "it wasn't like Robert to do such a thing. The police report says suicide, but if you knew him like I did, it was impossible."

I thought it would take some time to open the discussion, but she had jumped to the heart of the matter. "So, what happened?" I asked.

"They, BMP Capital, put an inordinate amount of pressure on him, but still he didn't give in."

"What kind of pressure?"

"A lot of things. First he signed a Non-Disclosure Agreement with them and then realized there was this crazy exclusivity clause in the agreement. Robert was a fighter. He challenged them on it."

"What was the background?"

"The background?"

"Yes, how did he get involved with them and what was their response when he didn't like the NDA?"

"It was complicated." Her eyes turned away.

"Like how?"

"Well, it actually started before he signed the NDA. It was a time when he and I weren't sure about getting married and we had a cooling off period. There were some tensions between us." She took a deep breath and faced me. "Let me cut to the chase. When we decided to cool things for a while he started to see another woman. He lost perspective and somehow I think the woman was mixed up with BMP Capital. But, I can't prove that."

"What was she like?" I felt it was a replay of the story with James Robinson last night.

Her eyes squinted. "You mean her personality or her looks?" She asked.

"Her looks. Physically."

"Why is that relevant?"

"I'm just trying to put one and one together. Remember that BMP Capital is currently in the process of trying to, ah; court me, you might say. At least I'm trying to determine if that's the case."

"Oh, I see." She raised her eyebrows. "I saw her once and we got into a verbal cat fight. She was just taller than me, dark hair, olive complexion, and hot. I mean really hot."

It was strange for me to think of a girl describing another girl that way, as 'hot' especially one that was seeing her fiancé, but this was the Bay Area where life was different than L.A.

"Does that description sound familiar?" She asked.

"No. Well, some. Hot, yes, but more like five ten or five eleven."

"They sure know how to pick them. Perfect match-makers," she said.

"I'm not sure the girl I'm seeing is involved with them. What drove Robert to do what he did… to end his life?"

"I tell you he didn't do it."

"How do you know that?" I asked.

"Because he wouldn't do such a thing. All I know is that he was going to meet with this Al Manchini character, and the next thing we learn is that Robert's body is floating in the bay, on May twenty-eighth, a little over three months ago."

"Did anyone see him jump?"

"No. I tell you he didn't kill himself."

"So, you think Manchini did it?"

"Probably not him, as he had a pretty tight alibi. But definitely some of his thugs."

"That's a pretty hard accusation," I said. "You need some proof."

"It just really bothers me that I don't have any." She raised the palms of her hands in resignation.

"Did Robert ever talk about the contract he signed with BMP Capital?"

"The NDA?" She asked.

"No. The VC contract."

"He never mentioned it."

I asked, "Yet after his death that's what they used to proclaim their right to manage the company, right?"

"Yes. In the case that the founder became incapacitated or died the venture capitalist has the right to inject its own management team, to protect their investment so they affirm. And that's what they did. Then they stripped the assets and sold them off, quick and dirty."

I thought of something. "Is it possible there is a photo of the girl Robert was seeing?"

"The girl?"

"From BMP Capital, the 'hot' one."

She raised one side of her lip. "Robert took photos of everything and everyone. There could be a photo of her here in Robert's things. Just a minute."

She left and several minutes later came back holding several photos and handed them to me. It was true; the girl was like a Latin beauty. "Do you think I could borrow these?"

"As far as I'm concerned you can pour acid on them and flush them down the toilet."

"Yes, when you consider what happened I can understand." I put the photos in my shirt pocket. "Do you have any advice for me?"

Her fist tightened. "Don't let them do to you what they did to Robert."

CHAPTER 39

On Highway 101 not far from the San Jose airport the engine of the Chevrolet just stopped running, as if it ran out of gas. I put it into neutral, drifted over to the shoulder and rolled a while until it stopped. After lifting the hood I took my canvas shoulder bag and started walking along the side of the freeway in the direction of the airport.

I held out a thumb and it only took a couple of minutes for someone to pick me up, a Mexican in an old pickup truck. He was a gardener and the truck had a lawnmower in the back along with an assortment of rakes and brooms. He seemed surprised that I spoke Spanish so fluently and asked if I had grown up in Mexico, thinking I might have been the child of American missionaries.

He kindly drove me to the airport.

I was late for checking in and the security seemed to take forever. While waiting in the security line I called the car rental agency and spoke with the same guy who picked me up two days ago. I told him where he could find the Chevrolet.

"Why didn't you put gas in it?" he asked.

"Yesterday you said the gas tank was full and I only drove up to past Redwood City. The car should still be more than half full."

"That can't be true," he said. "What is the mileage?"

"The odometer is broken."

"We're going to have to charge your credit card for having to pick up the car," he said.

"You do and I'll kick your ass," I said.

A woman in front of me in the line turned around and looked at me with a stern face.

"We'll see," he said and the phone went dead.

I could see that my cheap rental car was now going to be expensive, and sure I could contest the credit card billing, but it was just another hassle added to my ever growing list.

I went though security and saw that my flight was boarding, but made one last check of my voicemail before having to turn off the cell phone. There was only one message from Al Manchini.

"Hank, I'm serious. You better call me today. Things are going to heat up."

I turned off the cell phone and was the last person to board the flight. It taxied out and accelerated down the runway and I was thinking how little muscle there was in the threat from Al. My apartment was burned down and there was nothing else they could do to me.

Then I started to think about how they might have found out personal information about me. He seemed to know I needed a lawyer. How did he learn about the thing with King-Fu? What else did he know about me? Was Janie involved? She knew quite a bit about me and had even met my foster parents, Clyde and Rochelle. And then a horrible thought went through my mind. Would they go after them next?

I felt helpless. I reached into my canvas shoulder bag, took out my cell phone, turned it on and started to punch in Clyde's telephone number.

Down the aisle I saw a cabin attendant quickly moving in my direction. She said, "You can't do that!"

CHAPTER 40

"It's an emergency, life and death." I pleaded.

"Cell phones are to be turned off inside the aircraft," she commanded.

I continued tapping in Clyde's number.

"Sir you are committing a Federal offense. If you want to make a call there is one in the back of the aircraft."

"Okay," I said, getting up from my aisle seat and heading to the back of the plane.

People were wide eyed, like a terrorist had taken over the airplane. "What's wrong," I heard a woman ask the flight attendant.

On a wall in the back of the plane I found the telephone. I lifted it and saw that I had to swipe my credit card. Quickly I did it and then called Jake.

He said, "Man, I'm glad you called. Where are you?"

"On an airplane on my way back to L.A. Can you help with a potential problem. I think someone might try to do something to Clyde and Rochelle."

"Something happened," he said. His voice didn't sound right. "About an hour ago someone threw a Molotov cocktail through their front window. Clyde was there and put it out, but their living room is burned up. I'm on my way over there right now."

"I knew it, I knew it. I'm so stupid," I said.

"What do you mean?"

"If I'd been thinking quicker we might have prevented it."

"You knew about this?"

"Not specifically, but I'm getting heavy handed threats from a venture capital firm."

"What are you talking about, man?"

"It's complex. I've found some scary information in Silicon Valley. I'll update you when I get to L.A., but can you stay with Clyde and Rochelle and look out for them. Maybe you can get Delay and Rayshawn over there with you for some backup?"

"You're serious," he stated.

"At this point I really don't know what to think. Just look out for Clyde and Rochelle."

We hung up and I called Robert Campbell and advised him to improve the security around Campbell Labs. Somehow I didn't think that BMP Capital would push it that far. TechZip was legally registered at the Campbell Labs address and all the company knowledge was really there. After my meetings with the people in Silicon Valley I could see that BMP Capital's game was hostile takeovers of startup companies. It didn't make sense they would burn down Campbell Labs. Yet, if they had taken my PC and the binders with all the technical details related to my system and patent application, they really didn't need anything at Campbell Labs. They had everything they needed to run TechZip. A growing sense of hopelessness began to fill me.

I went back to my seat and the eyes of everyone on the airplane followed me. I slumped into my seat angry for what had happened to Clyde and Rochelle, feeling weak, wondering what I could really do about BMP Capital. In fact I wasn't even sure they were the ones who were behind the fires, but everything pointed in that direction.

Now all I could do was sit still and wait until the airplane landed, but what were my options? Once we landed I would track down Detective Grady to have his expert look at a couple of signatures, but where would I go from there?

The phone calls at the back of the plane had cost me a bundle. My cash position was dropping too quickly.

* * *

As soon as I got off the airplane I turned on my cell phone on and called Detective Grady. He said he was busy but that a Ms. Perkins, a handwriting expert, was willing to help me. It was at the main L.A.P.D. headquarters in downtown L.A. I figured it would take me forty-five minutes to get over there if the traffic was kind to me. He said he would call to let her know I was coming.

Then I called Jake.

"Are you at their place?" I asked.

"Yeah. Their living room is a mess. Luckily Clyde had fire extinguishers because of the requirements for running foster homes. Without that the entire house would have burned."

"How are they doing?"

"They're shook up, but you know them. They've got resolve and now their neighbors are helping to clean up the place. Everywhere in the house smells like smoke and they're going to have to renovate the living room. It's a mess."

"Were the police there?"

"They just left. They seemed resigned, like it's an everyday occurrence in this part of the world."

"Did anyone see it happen?"

"Some neighbors saw a car pull up in front, a black guy with his face covered gets out, lights the rag in the bottle and then throws it through the window. Then he gets back in the car and it speeds away."

"Any idea who it was?"

"The car was a black Cadillac, new. Now who drives a new Cadillac in this part of the world?" he asked.

"Drug dealers?"

"That's what we're assuming," Jake stated.

"You think it was King-Fu's people."

"That's our starting point. They're about the only ones stupid enough to do something like this in broad daylight."

"But why would they do it?"

"My only guess is that it's because Clyde and Rochelle are connected to you and me, and they are just making a statement. In any case, Delay and Rayshawn have hit the streets and are looking for information."

"Would you let me know if they find anything? I'll try and get over to Clyde and Rochelle's later on, and I hope your offer for a place to stay is still good."

"You bet. Where are you going now?" he asked.

"To meet with someone at L.A.P.D. headquarters."

"You at Cop H.Q.? You're kidding!" he said.

We hung up. I took the airport shuttle bus to the parking area, got my Jeep and drove over to L.A.P.D. headquarters. It was a massive building and I felt nervous when I walked in the front door. For my entire life I had considered cops to be enemies, and even though I didn't think I had done anything major, just being here made me edgy.

I went to the front desk and was directed to Ms. Perkin's office. I walked down a hall and entered a room that only had the word 'Laboratory' on the door.

Inside was a room with several tables filled with microscopes, electronic devices, computers, beeker jars, and various types of scientific instruments. There was a woman looking into a microscope and when she heard me enter the room she stood up. She was thin, wore dark rimmed glasses and a gray dress.

"Excuse me, but I'm looking for Ms. Perkins," I said.

"Detective Grady informed me. Do you have the documents?" Her back was ramrod straight and she reminded me of a strict schoolteacher.

"Yes, Just a couple of signed contracts." I pulled them from my canvas bag and turned to the signature pages. "I'm not an expert, but something seem odd. Can you check it out?"

Ms. Perkins took them from my hands and stated, "Photocopies."

I nodded.

"And these are part of a crime investigation?"

"It may have something to do with Detective Grady's case, arson on my apartment."

"I can't really work on anything unless it is part of a formal investigation," she said, as she moved over to a table. She took off her glasses and put on some special kind of goggles and held the pages in front of a bright light. Then she overlaid the two signatures and looked at them for a while. She took the goggles off and put the glasses back on and went to a microscope and began to examine the signatures. Then she scanned the contracts and began to move the signatures around on the computer monitor.

As she worked she started to talk. "You know that Detective Grady gets involved in some of the strangest cases. For a long time he was one of the top homicide detectives on the L.A.P.D and then his partner got shot and died when they were investigating a case. Somehow he got into a row with his Captain and called her a 'Femi-Nazi' and then he was reassigned to Arson, the 'fire-patrol' as we call it. But even with this new assignment his cases seem to take on a life of their own."

I stood there patiently waiting. It was true. Behind this case was something much bigger and more sinister than burning down a garage.

Finally she turned to me and said, "Is it possible to get the originals?"

"They're in Redwood City."

"Near San Francisco?" she asked.

"Yes."

"There's definitely something fishy here. Certain things have unusually extreme precision, like an exact replica, but there are also some subtle differences, like the pen pressure being stronger on the right loops of several letters. This all indicates that one of the signatures is a forgery. Of course these are photocopies and I'd only be able to verify this if I had the original signed documents."

"I think I could get them if you think it's worthwhile."

"Absolutely. It's always of interest to discover anomalies."

"Then I'll try and get it to you as quick as possible."

"I'm here tomorrow, off on Sunday and then back in on Monday," she said.

"I may be able to get them to you by Monday." Then I remembered the photo in my pocket and something I had read in a magazine. I asked, "Are you able to identify someone from a photo? I heard about some new technology used by the police."

"What do you mean?" She asked.

'I read somewhere that the police have a technology that's similar to fingerprint matching; only it's matching a photo or drawing of someone with photos in a database."

"Its part of our national criminal archives containing mug shots and other crime related photos. Everyone has a unique face, that is, the dimensions between eyes, ears, chin, and other reference points are different. The system compares those coordinates. The archive isn't complete, but it is growing."

I pulled the photo that Carole Gunnerson had given me of the girl who was seeing Robert Montet, who she suspected was from BMP Capital. "Is this of a good enough quality to be checked through that system?"

She held it next to a light. "Yes. It would work, but there is no guarantee that we would find a match."

"Could you try?" I asked.

"How is this linked to Detective Grady's case?"

"Maybe it's connected to someone who is starting some fires," I stated.

She looked at me suspiciously. "Does Detective Grady know about this?"

"Not yet. It just came up and I haven't had a chance to see him. But, I'll let him know."

She placed the photo on her scanner and then made a copy. She turned to me and said, "This may take a while, but I'm here until nine tonight. Call me before then or call on Monday." She handed me her business card.

"Thank you very much," I said.

I left the building and headed for my car.

I wasn't sure where the photo might lead, but what I had learned about the signatures frightened me deeply. If the pieces of the puzzle lined up it had to do with the dark car following me the other day. And it had to do with Al Manchini wanting to get together with me. They had my signature on the NDA and because of that they actually didn't need me. All they had to do was copy my name to their standard contract and TechZip belonged to them. One line in the contract read, "If the founder becomes incapacitated or in the event of the founder's death, BMP Capital has the right to assume management of the company."

I still didn't know how Janie Carlton fit into this, nor Thomas Bennett, but I had ideas. I also imagined a small obituary in the L.A. Times, *Hank Morgan was a former Marine, a graduate of UCLA and the founder of TechZip. Because of mounting personal pressure he jumped off a tall bridge and killed himself. He was a real loser.* The Times' version would be worded more politically correct and they definitely wouldn't include the sentence: *He jumped off the bridge with a little assistance from Al Manchini and friends.*

For the first time I understood what they intended to do to me and I was terrified. I didn't want to end up floating in the water like Robert Montet.

CHAPTER 41

My plan was to go down to Clyde and Rochelle's house after visiting Ms. Perkins, but I went over to Culver City instead. I wanted to make sure that Robert Campbell had enough security around Campbell Labs. If Al Mancini had my PC and company records, the only backup was at Campbell Labs. If Campbell Labs went up in flames, then Al would be holding all the cards. Robert's life could also be in danger.

I parked my Jeep in the parking lot and went inside. Robert was still there.

"What's going on?" He asked.

I gave him a summary of what I had discovered in the Bay Area and from Ms. Perkins.

"This is wild," he exclaimed. "It's a fact that some VC's are ruthless, more like vulture-capitalists than venture-capitalists, but this is too much. You think they would actually kill someone to take their company?"

I said, "I know it sounds bizarre, but that's the only conclusion I could come up with. Of course the original signatures on the two contracts needs to be verified by Ms. Perkins, but that's what it's leading to."

"Even if forgery can be verified, it still doesn't prove they threw the guy over the bridge," he affirmed.

"Sure, it's circumstantial, but when you talked with his mother and fiancée, you just get the impression that he was a tough little guy who would never take that alternative. It just wasn't in his character."

"Still, there is no proof."

"Okay, point taken, but we better not be naïve," I stated. "Is there enough security around this place?"

"I asked my security company to get a full time person over here, rather than just passing by every few hours. I told them I received a threat and it was better to be safe than sorry."

I looked across the room and couldn't imagine it going up in flames. The value of the loss here would be in multiples of what I had lost in my apartment. I noticed that Freddy the communications guy was at his computer. He saw me looking and waved me over.

"I did the research you asked for," he said. "She's not a student there."

"Are you sure?"

"There is a Carlton at Vassar, but not a Janie or Jane Carlton. There's a Ms. Carlton who's been working in their library for about fifty years."

"How did you find that out?"

"Most universities have pitiful security on their databases, especially for something like lists of students. There's always a backdoor and Vassar is no exception."

"Like how?"

"Just about every service in any university has a list of students. You name it, the administration office, the library, the security office, the cafeteria; one or more is likely to have public access to the list. I can guarantee that she isn't a student there, unless she goes by another name."

"Thanks Freddy," I said.

I went back to Robert and reiterated my concern about his safety and the safety of Campbell Labs. He said he would make sure there were people constantly on site and that the security company kept constant surveillance. His phone rang and it was Sharlee. She spoke with Robert about some details on the beta test and then wanted to talk with me.

"Glad you're back in L.A.," she said.

"It's good to be back." Her voice made me feel good. "How was your week?"

"It's not finished. I'm still over at Unipac."

"You're still there?"

"Yes, I'm just checking out some of the reports from the system and then there's another meeting."

"I can't believe you're still there. This is dedication above and beyond the call of duty."

She laughed. "Honesty, I really enjoyed the week. Makes me wonder if I should be going into public administration."

"Well I hope not for a while. What's the meeting you're going to?"

"Well, it's not exactly a meeting. Mr. Oliver, ah, Sam is in L.A. to attend an event tomorrow. He's here with his wife and they stopped into the factory this afternoon where he gave a speech to everyone. I went to the speech and he saw me. We talked and he and his wife invited me out to dinner this evening."

"To dinner… with Sam Oliver?"

"Yes."

"I can't believe it. You're running in important circles."

She chuckled. "It will be a simple restaurant, so his wife said."

"I bet. A billionaire and his wife take you to dinner. It will probably outdo where Al Manchini took us."

"I hope not. He gave me the creeps."

I paused for a moment. "Your instincts were good," I said, remembering how she said she had her doubts.

"I hope you won't have anything more to do with him," she stated.

"Me too, but it might be more serious than we think."

"What does that mean?" she asked.

"He may have had something to do with the fire at my apartment. I found out some things on my trip north."

"That can't possibly be. What would he gain from that?"

"Trying to prove who is the boss, and some other things." I thought about how they had used the fire as a camouflage to steal my PC and company records.

"That's incredible. I don't understand it, but you will be cautious in dealing with him, wont you?"

"For sure. Enjoy your dinner with Sam Oliver," I said.

"I'm a bit nervous."

"You'll do just fine," I reassured.

We hung up and I was amazed how Sharlee had been able to strike up a friendship with the legendary Sam Oliver. She totally surprised me. Somehow I still saw her as the skinny young girl who was always there by my side. Now she passed me by. In the bottom of my heart I was proud of her.

I went to the desk Sharlee had been using and spent a few minutes considering my next move and decided not to go directly to Clyde and Rochelle's. I needed some information first.

Robert and I walked out of Campbell Labs. In front there was a car from the security company with a man inside. Robert walked over to talk with him and I walked to the end of the row where my Jeep was parked. Next to it was a dark car with tinted windows and when I approached it the window on the rider's side came down, slightly.

"Hank, my friend. Where have you been?" It was Al Manchini. Because of the tinted glass I could only see part of the driver's face. But something about him seemed familiar.

"Busy," I said.

"I'm so sorry to hear about the fire. You know we can help you out."

"Don't need that kind of help," I said.

"What do you mean?"

"I've decided to do it on my own."

"You're being unreasonable. We can provide you with financing, lawyers, and fire insurance, whatever you need. You can see that it'd be helpful."

"Don't need it."

"In any case, we still have the NDA. What shall we do about that?"

"Stick it," I said.

"Now, Hank. That's not a good attitude. How bout we get together and solve this amicably?"

I assumed they wouldn't try something hostile here, with the security guy close by. Al Manchini would want a secure alibi when they made their move.

"Don't need to meet," I said.

"Look Hank. Let's just save you some troubles. We don't want anything more to happen to you. Why don't we get together privately in a situation more conducive to talking and then we can dissolve the agreement like gentlemen?"

"Okay. When and where?" I asked.

"How about tomorrow at ten o'clock at our offices?"

"Where are your offices?"

He handed me a business card with the address.

"Okay. See you then," I said.

"You won't regret it Hank." His window went up.

Al Manchini's car drove off and I felt myself shaking. It took all my willpower to hold myself back. My basic instinct was to grab his head and yank it through the window and leave his body behind. But, I couldn't do it. It wasn't the time or the place.

In fact, I wasn't sure what to do. They held every advantage over me.

But with maybe a gamble I could at least try.

CHAPTER 42

I drove on the I-10 to West L.A and exited south on Soto Street. It was just before nine o'clock and I suddenly remembered that I had to call Ms. Perkins at the L.A.P.D. I took out her business card and dialed her number.

"Perkins," she answered.

"Hello Ms. Perkins. This is Hank Morgan. You said I should call you back before nine for the information on the photo. Did you find out anything?"

"Did you speak with Detective Grady?" She asked.

"Not yet. He said he was off duty this weekend."

"It's still Friday. I gave him a call and he's still working."

"Then I'll try and call him," I said with my most reassuring voice.

"You better," she demanded.

"Don't worry, I will. Did the photo turn up anything?"

"In fact it did. Her name was Tina Bernardo. She has a couple of entries into the criminal database. Six months ago she was arrested for prostitution in San Francisco. Three months ago her body was found on an access road next to the bay just south of San Francisco airport. Her hands were bound behind her back and she was shot in the back two times with a .38 caliber weapon. No one has been apprehended in the case."

I was shocked. "She's dead? What was the date they found her?"

"June third. Why do you ask?"

"I'm just trying to put a timeline together." Carole Gunnerson had told me that Robert Montet's body was found on May twenty eighth. Surely Robert couldn't have killed Tina Bernardo. If she was working for BMP Capital could they have done that to her, just to eliminate a witness?

"Mr. Morgan, you better call Detective Grady," Ms. Perkins commanded. "How can a falsified signature on a contract signed in Palo Alto and the murder of a young woman near the San Francisco Airport have anything to do with suspected arson at your home in

Venice Beach?"

"I'm not sure."

"Then you'd better at least talk it through with Detective Grady."

"I'll give him a call."

We hung up and somehow I wished I had a photo of Janie to give to Ms. Perkins. It disturbed me to know that Janie had lied to me by saying she attended Vassar and was a history and pre-law student. Who was she and was her name really Janie Carlton? Seeing the pattern of how BMP Capital was using women to seduce men, either as a means of blackmail or intelligence gathering, it seemed that was exactly Janie's game. How else had they learned so much about me?

In fact, it was blatant intelligence gathering. From our first date she had wanted to visit my apartment and when I finally took her there I showed her where all my important records were kept. She had taken an unusual interest in TechZip and asked numerous questions about the company. I had also told her about Martha and they paid Martha to come and see me in an effort to weaken my emotions. Janie also knew about Clyde and Rochelle, even having been to their place. She was at Brother's Club when I attacked King-Fu, and after that this high-powered lawyer visits King-Fu in the hospital. Why would the lawyer even care?

Looking at it now, the threats of a court trial seemed nothing more than an effort to put pressure on me, to make me want to accept their contractual offer and their legal assistance. In a few short days Janie had invaded my life and seduced me, exactly like the women who had seduced James Robinson and Robert Montet. Did all the other founders on the BMP Capital list have a similar experience?

Are men really that vulnerable? Shamefully I had to admit that I was weak, naively lured by an encounter that promised excitement and 'love', if you could call it that?

Ms. Perkins said that Tina Bernardo was arrested on prostitution. Is that where BMP Capital found these women? Is that what Janie really was? It sickened me to think so, but I had grown up in an environment where that was a reality in so many women's lives.

There was one thing I didn't understand when I thought about my time with Janie. The night when I drove her back to her car after the incident at Brother's Club she had said to herself, "I can't go on with this." What did she mean by that? I wish I could find out more, but there's no way to know how to find her.

The awful thing was to think what happened when BMP Capital

was finished with them. Did they all end up with their hands tied behind them, shot them in the back and left in some bushes to die? Even though I was feeling anger toward Janie, it angered me even more to think how she might end up. I didn't want that. Their only option now was to get rid of me and then take over TechZip. Then they would kill Janie to eliminate any evidence, and the thought of that made me shudder.

★ ★ ★

I parked my Jeep outside the Mexican bar and went inside. Jacko was at the same table where I had met him before. One of the guys with him still had bandages across his nose.

When Jacko saw me he waved his guy to leave. "Morgan, *amigo*, please sit."

I sat down. "How are your guys doing?" I asked.

"They will survive. But this only adds to your reputation."

"I was just defending myself. You would have done the same."

"It's true *amigo*, but you have my respect."

He ordered a beer for me and I was thankful. We clicked beer bottles.

"Did you find anything," I asked.

"You will be interested," he said.

I took out my checkbook to write out a check for the amount we had agreed and he reached out across the table and put his hand on mine. "Wait," he said.

"Why? You didn't get any information?" I asked.

He smiled. "We got what you wanted."

"What did you find?"

"I visited Lola at the house in Malibu as a lost delivery boy. I spoke to her in Spanish hoping no one would understand and I quickly found out that she does not have a visa for the U.S. That gave me some leverage."

"They've hired an undocumented worked, *sin papeles*?" I asked.

He laughed. "What's so special about that? There are millions in this country."

"Okay, you're right. What did she say?"

"First that they never let her off the property. She's worked there for over a year, gets minimum wage and sends the money home to her family in Central America."

"Did she tell you anything about the people who live there?"

"For sure. She took me to a place by the house where the camera could not watch us. And then once she started to talk she didn't stop. She hasn't spoken Spanish with anyone for a long time. She said that there are always one or two security guards on the property with other 'rough men' as she called them coming and going."

"Does she know who owns the place?"

"She's not sure, but the man in charge seems to be a lawyer. He is there about once a week and gives orders."

"What's his name?"

"Thomas Bennett."

I stiffened.

"You seem to know him," Jacko said.

"It all fits. He has been threatening to sue me." My mind was racing. "And Janie, what did Lola say about her?"

"Janie stays there sometimes."

"Does she know anything about her?"

"Not really. Janie always stays at the guesthouse is about all she could tell me. Oh yes, and that the men are always bossing her around, especially Thomas Bennett."

"Bossing her around?"

"Yes. It sounded to me like she is working for them."

"What about the guesthouse? Janie didn't take me down there."

"Lola cleans it once a week and there's always someone watching her. She isn't allowed into some of the rooms."

"Why not?"

"She doesn't know." He looked me straight in the eyes. "It's strange, isn't it."

I nodded my head. "For sure. Did you learn anything else?"

"I didn't have much time and she started to get nervous. They have security cameras everywhere and she is afraid of them."

"Thanks," I said. "And the car. Did you find out who owns it?"

Jacko smiled. "We know."

"Who is it?"

"The Ferrari was owned by a company."

"A company?" I asked.

"Uh huh. A company named BMP Capital."

"What?"

He looked at me with inquisitive eyes. "Is there a problem?"

"More than you know." Pieces of the puzzle were rapidly falling in place and it confirmed to me that Janie was part of this scam to take over TechZip. "How did you manage to find that out?"

"One of my guys staked out the house with the address you gave me in Beverley Hills. He saw the beautiful *chica* drive away and he followed her to an office building near Rodeo Drive and into an underground parking. Then we found out."

I thought a moment about something he said. "You mentioned that the Ferrari 'was' owned by a company. What do you mean?"

"It is such a beautiful car. It is a pity that it has been taken by someone."

"Taken?"

"There is a rumor that it is on its way to a country south of the U.S. border where it will be enjoyed." He laughed.

"You took the car!"

"My friend, I do not admit to nothing. It is just a rumor, but let me say that you do not owe me any money."

"That's incredible. Thanks, I appreciate it."

"And many of us around here are thankful for what you did to Romero Rodriguez. He was one bad *hombre*."

"I was angry," I said.

"We understand. Many people were angry with him, but they were afraid."

I thought back. Two of my fifteen-year-old friends had died because of the bad heroin he had given to them in an effort to get them hooked, so they would work for him. Besides them Romero had killed innocent people in the community. He was twenty-five and I was fifteen and I had taken a lead pipe and almost beat him to death. It took him a year and a half to walk again, and then because he didn't have a visa, the U.S. Border Patrol sent him back to Venezuela. Some say his superiors shot him when he got back there. That's the reason the Social Services moved me to another part of town. The fact is I had beaten his head to a bloody pulp.

What could I say? "Thanks Jacko. You have my respect. Let's keep in touch. Maybe someday we can have a meal together at Mama Caterina's."

I put out my hand and he shook it.

"Good luck *amigo*," he said.

CHAPTER 43

I drove west on I-10 was feeling sick about what Jacko had told me. It confirmed that Thomas Bennett and BMP Capital were connected and Janie was right in the middle of it. They had used her to get into my life and into my head just like they had used women to invade the lives of all the other entrepreneurs they had worked with. Through that they found out everything they could about the entrepreneur or set him up through blackmail and that gave them tremendous leverage.

In my case they knew I was attending the technology fair in San Jose and Al Manchini showed up and got me to sign the NDA, the first step in taking over TechZip. It is likely they were the ones who burned down my apartment and took my company records. The lawsuit from King-Fu was another effort to get me to crack. The night adventures with Janie broke down my ability to think straight and clouded my judgment.

In effect they were working to gain a signed venture capital agreement and then to take over my company, for whatever it was worth. Even without the venture capital agreement, the NDA was enough for them to take control, if Robert Montet's case was an example.

Why didn't I see what they were doing? I was so taken up by my obsession of Janie that I was blinded even to some obvious details. For instance, she told me she was twenty-six years old. She also said she was an undergraduate at Vassar. For sure there are some twenty-six year old undergraduates, but that should have raised some questions in my mind. It didn't even register.

It made me feel violated and angry, but what could I do about it? There was nothing I could prove. None of the other entrepreneurs who had been pushed to the side by BMP Capital would say anything or back me up because they lived lives of fear. Even if they did, BMP Capital had an army of powerful lawyers who would defend them.

I wondered what I could do and thought about going over to Clyde and Rochelle's, or to Jake's place, but decided I needed more information. In spite of the fact that Janie had used me and lied to me, I was horrified to think what they could do to her, the same as Tina Bernardo. When I thought of Janie I realized I didn't know that much about her and wondered if there was any way to learn more.

I felt I needed more information before knowing if I had any alternatives.

I pulled off the freeway and made my way to Rodeo Drive and parked in front of the building where I had seen Janie park the Ferrari in the underground garage. In my bag I pulled out the printout from the website of Bennett, Medici and Associates. It was their building.

The night we went to Brother's Club, she asked me to leave her there. It was a tactical error on her part, because it enabled me to make the connection between her and Bennett. Maybe she was so shaken up by the incident at Brother's Club that she wasn't thinking straight?

I was opening the door to get out of my Jeep when my cell phone rang.

"Hank Morgan," I said.

"Detective Grady here."

"Ah, hello," I said.

"Perkins told me about the signatures on the agreements and the female victim in the Bay Area. She said you said you would call me. What's going on?"

"You told me you were not working on the weekend," I stated.

"It's still Friday," he said, "Well, just. When we talked earlier today you said you might have information relating to the arson of your apartment, some signatures, so I sent you to Perkins. What's going on?"

I didn't know what to tell him. "I'm not sure, but I think someone might be trying to take over my company."

There was silence for a moment. "And they burn your apartment down? What's that got to do with it?"

"They put pressure on entrepreneurs."

"So they burn your place down and then take your company. What's your company worth?"

"Not much. It's a startup." I was beginning to feel stupid.

"So they go through all the trouble of burning your place down for something that's not worth anything?"

"Ah, yeah."

The line went silent again. "And Tina Bernardo. How does she fit into this?"

"I think they killed her."

"Now, why's that?"

"She was involved in an entrepreneur's death. They killed him too."

"Who did this?" He asked.

"BMP Capital."

"Perkins gave me the name. It was on the contracts you gave her.

And the falsified signature of Robert Montet was also on the contracts. It appears he jumped off the Golden Gate Bridge."

"He was pushed off," I said.

"No kidding. How do you know that?"

"His fiancée told me."

"How does she know?"

"She said so."

"Good proof," he said. "Is that why you flew up to San Jose, to talk with her?"

"Yes, partially."

"Look Hank, this all seems a number of loose connected assumptions. Why don't you back off and let the professionals take care of the investigations? You can't start taking a whole bunch of unrelated events and imagine they are linked. You need hard evidence."

"Then do your job," I said. He was making me frustrated.

"Give me a lead," he said.

"You can start with Bennett, Medici and Associates," I said.

"Who are they?"

"Some lawyers potentially linked with BMP Capital. They're stealing people's companies."

"Where are you going with this?"

"You asked for a lead and I gave it to you."

"Hank, I'd advise you to back off from this. It all sounds very disjointed."

"Check it out. If you don't then I will. I gotta go," I said.

"Let's calm down a bit. You stay in touch with me, okay?"

"Okay."

We hung up. That conversation made me feel awful and I knew I appeared to be an idiot in the eyes of Detective Grady. In his mind these were all unrelated connections. I needed to get more evidence to build substance to my arguments.

I walked across the street to the office building and went inside. A security guard was sitting at the front desk so I went up to him. He was reading a magazine and looked up at me.

"What do you need?" He asked.

"I'm looking for a company," I stated. "Is BMP Capital in this building? They gave me their address and I lost it."

"No one's here right now," he said.

"But an Al, ah, somebody told me to come here to meet him."

"Al Manchini?"

I smiled. "Yeah, that's him."

"He ain't here."

"Do you know where I can find him?"

"No idea. Why don't you come back on Monday?" His eyes drifted back to the magazine.

"Okay, thanks, I will." I looked above his head and there was a security camera pointed at me.

I turned and quickly walked from the building not wanting to confront them here. There was a question gnawing at my brain.

CHAPTER 44

I drove north on Pacific Coast highway now certain that BMP Capital and the lawyer Thomas Bennett were operating together. The security guard knew Al Manchini. As stupid as I had sounded when talking with Detective Grady there was in fact a connection, but what could I do to prove it?

Somehow I felt that Janie had the answer. If I could just find her and talk with her she might help me. Or would she?

The worse thought was what happened to Tina Bernardo and I wondered if I could get to Janie before she would meet a similar end.

I got to Malibu and drove into a section of town full of apartment buildings remembering the very first time I ever saw Janie when she came down to the beach. Mike the beach bum knew her. He had called out her name and said something like "where's the party."

Mike was a perpetual party guy, spending all day at the beach playing volleyball and the evenings attending parties wherever he got invited, or just having parties at his place when nothing else was happening. He seemed to have a string of girlfriends.

He used to hang out around the lifeguard stand sometimes and we would talk. He knew everyone in Malibu, which parties were happening, who was sleeping with whom and what girls were available.

Mike lived in an apartment a couple of blocks away from the beach, where all the units were full of singles. Every night at ten o'clock there was a disco beat in the air, doors open, and people roaming from one apartment to another.

I parked the Jeep and went into the apartment complex. It was square shaped with all the apartments facing into the center with a swimming pool in the middle. It was just after midnight and music was thumping from a couple of places. The door to Mike's place was open so I walked in. Three guys were sitting on a long couch watching an action movie on a TV, beer cans on the table in front of them. One of them turned when I walked in.

"Is Mike around?" I asked.

"Not here." He turned to back to the movie.

"Know where he is?" I asked.

"Busy," he said.

I walked in front of the TV to block their view. "Where?"

"Hey," one of the yelled. "Get out of the way."

I reached down to the table, picked up the remote, turned down the volume and went back in front of the TV. "Where's Mike?"

The guy sitting in the middle got up and took a step toward me. The guy on the far end said, "Jimmy, back off. That's the lifeguard that took out the six bikers down at the beach."

He stopped and then took a step back. In reality it was only three, but that's how information travels.

"Where's Mike?" I asked.

The one on the end said, "Apartment sixteen."

"Okay, thanks." I tossed the remote to him.

He caught it. The three of them watched me leave the room and then I heard the TV volume increase.

I found apartment sixteen on the upper floor and knocked on the door. There wasn't an answer so I turned the handle and went inside. Soft music was playing, candles were burning and some kind of strange incense filled the air, mixed with the sweet smell of marijuana.

Mike was on the couch with a girl. He was down to his boxer shorts and she had a similar configuration, female version. They were entangled together. I walked over to the CD player and turned the volume down.

"Mike," I said.

He sat up. "Ahhh. What are you doing here? Man you scared me."

The girl sat up and held her hands over her breasts.

"Need to ask you a question," I said. I walked into the light so he could see me.

"Hank?"

"Yeah."

"What are you doing here? Can't you see I'm, ah, busy."

"Uh huh. I just got an urgent question and then you can get back to it," I said.

"Who is this guy?" the girl asked.

"It's okay," Mike said. "Can you do me a favor and go into the bedroom for a minute?"

"No. I don't like this. Can you ask him to leave," she said.

I said, "I'm not leaving. I need to ask Mike a question."

"Mike, if you're a man you will get rid of him. He's uninvited in my apartment."

"This isn't your apartment," Mike said. "You're living downstairs."

"I am?"

"Yeah," Mike said.

She reached to the floor and put on a t-shirt and stormed out the front door. Mike raised his hands and said, " You ruined it."

"She'll get over it. Answer my question and you can pick up where it ended."

"What's the question man," he asked.

I sat down across from him. "You remember a little over a week ago when you were at the beach and Janie showed up. You called out her name and joked with her about a party. What do you know about her?"

"Janie Carlton?"

I nodded.

"Something, but not everything. Grew up in Beverly Hills. Her father was some rich guy and her mother drank herself to death. Father went bankrupt and shot himself. Happened when Janie was back east at some college."

"Vassar?" I asked.

"Maybe, but it could have been something different. Anyway, Janie was always a party girl, even in high school. Rumor was she wasn't doing well in college because of her party life. With the father gone and everything lost, she went to dancing, first Las Vegas, but because she knew the scene out here she got some jobs at some clubs in Hollywood."

"And you've seen her around?" I asked.

"Not a lot. I rarely get invited to the kind of parties she goes to. Different class, but sometimes I'd see her."

"Who was she with?"

"Different rich guys," he said.

"Did you know any of those rich guys?"

"Not really. A couple of older ones."

"How'd she make her money?" I asked.

"Living with them, maybe. I don't know. Just look at her. She's just about the hottest chick I've ever seen."

"Giving favors?" I asked.

"I suspected high class escort," he said.

"What was she doing hanging around me?" I asked.

Mike laughed. "I wondered. That was strange. You're one lucky dude. What's going on?"

"Nothing," I said. "Just kind of a funny friendship. What else can you tell me?"

"That's about it, other than she's one smart chick, as well as the looks." He looked around the apartment. "Is that it? You kind-of interrupted me. I better go back and find the lady."

"Thanks," I said.

We walked out of apartment sixteen together and walked down the steps. Mike just wore his boxer shorts and went into another apartment.

I got into my Jeep feeling depressed and angry with Janie. A high-class hooker that had been used to get into my head, sent by BMP Capital, Al Manchini and Thomas Bennett, or whoever.

It wasn't the rich girl turned on by bad boy kind of thing, but something much more sinister.

CHAPTER 45

I parked my Jeep in the parking lot at Paradise Cove beach and began walking along the beach in the direction of Janie's beach house, if I could still call it that. It belonged to Thomas Bennett or BMP Capital I was sure.

It was dark, with just enough light for me to see the damp sand where it was easier to walk. The property was about half a mile down from the small pier at Paradise Cove.

I didn't know what to think as I walked along, feeling like an absolute fool for all that had happened, and it all happened so quickly. They knew what they were doing and were prepared for all contingencies. Now, if I were eliminated, they would own TechZip.

But then I got to thinking, was TechZip worth it? Based on the sale prices of the companies listed on their website, all the companies had been sold for tens or hundreds of millions. I knew that my project would be worth something some day, but couldn't imagine that it would ever be in that range. Yet, somehow they had the ability to pick winners and they were now after me. It was unfathomable to think that TechZip had that kind of value.

Up ahead I saw the beach house, set back on a small rise above the sand. It was two stories high with a long deck covering the length of the building. Large windows faced the ocean. I saw some lights on both upstairs and downstairs, but there were translucent curtains that made it impossible to see any details inside.

I walked across the dry sand until I came to a set of wooden stairs leading up to the deck. There was a metal barrier all around the bottom of the deck about eight feet high. A metal gate also eight feet was in front of the wooden stairs. I tried to open the gate, but it was locked.

Quietly I put my foot on the hinges of the door and climbed to the top of the gate and then dropped over the other side onto the wooden steps. It made a loud thump so I just waited for a couple of minutes to see if there was any movement of people.

The only sound I heard was the surf, waves crashing and then rumbling to shore. I tried to tiptoe up the steps but they creaked as I went up. I got to the deck and waited again and then crouched low and made my way over to one of the large windows and peered inside.

Through the a gap in the curtain I saw a large room and Janie was sitting on a large couch her knees bent and legs tucked to the side. She was reading a book. My heart jumped when I saw her, but I also felt anger. How could she sit there so tranquil while assisting them in stealing my company? She was a liar and I wanted to hate her for that, but my heart felt something different.

I went to the sliding glass door and knocked. Twenty seconds later the curtain moved back and Janie stood there with her eyes wide. She reached down and touched the latch and slid the door open.

"Hank. You shouldn't be here," she said.

"We need to talk."

"Not here."

"Can I come in?" I asked.

"Yes, quickly." She opened the door wider and I stepped into the living room. She put her finger horizontal to her lips and motioned me to go to a dark corner of the room where there was a little alcove next to the steps coming down from upstairs. We both sat down facing each other.

"Whisper," she said.

"What's going on?" I said with a low voice.

"It's not good for you to be here," she said.

"You're in pretty deep, you know that."

Her eyes became moist. "I know. I'm sorry."

"Were they ordering you?" I asked.

She nodded.

"That's why, the night we drove back after Brother's Club you said that you couldn't keep doing this. You were scared, right?"

"Yes, but they made me keep doing it. They threatened me. I was scared of them and frightened by you… your violence… your anger."

"And the nights we were together, when you visited me at eleven o'clock at my apartment, what do you say to that?"

She bowed her head. "I'm so sorry. I didn't know they were going to burn your place."

"But you made like you wanted me… loved me," I said.

"Hank, it's all mixed up, if you've been living a certain life and then a guy comes along who is very different from all the others, with them giving orders in the background, I don't know what to think or feel anymore. I've never met anyone like you."

"I'm scared for you Janie,"

She hesitated. "For me. Why?"

"For what they plan to do."

As I said out of the corner of my eyes I saw movement behind me and in the soft light there was reflection off some metal.

"Hold it." It was a man's voice.

I turned and was looking down the barrel of a gun.

CHAPTER 46

"Hey Frank, guess what I caught. Come here and bring your piece."

He was yelling upstairs and I was too far away from him to make a move. He held the gun with assurance like he knew how to use it.

A moment later Frank came running down the steps holding a gun with a silencer on the end. "Well, well, well," he said. He had a big smile.

"Didn't expect him to show up here," the first one said. "Shows yuh how bad the mouse wants the cheese." He looked to be in his mid forties, broad chest and was wearing a Hawaiian shirt, mostly big red flowers.

"Burt, what are you doing," Janie said. "Let him go."

Burt smiled. "Uh, uh. Thomas would like to speak with him. Over here," he said, waving his gun over to the large couch in the living room. "You too Janie. You sit next to him."

I slowly got up wondering if I could make a move on them, but they were both about four long steps away and separated from each other. If I got to one the other would have time to shoot. I also had Janie to worry about.

Janie and I went to the big couch and we sat down.

"What are you doing?" Janie said. "Why the guns?"

"Shut up," Frank said, pointing his gun at Janie. She moved in close to me.

Burt went over to the telephone, lifted it and made a call. "You better come down here. We got the Morgan kid," he said.

He hung up and then I remembered the guy who answered Janie's cell phone who called me "kid" and something was familiar with these two guys and I remembered. At the beach when I saved that little boy there were two guys in the crowd who said I was sitting on my ass and that I was a lazy bum. One wore a Hawaiian shirt. That was Burt. The other, bald, thick neck and muscular arms, built like a professional wrestler was Frank. They were watching me, looking for an opportunity to shake my emotions like they had been doing for days.

"What do you want?" I said.

"Shut up and wait," Burt said.

"What for?" I asked.

"Shoot her," Burt responded.

Frank pointed the gun at Janie and closed one eye. Janie pulled her knees up to her chest and leaned in next to me against my right shoulder..

"Stop I said. We'll wait."

"Good," Burt said.

Ten minutes later Thomas Bennett and Al Manchini entered the house. I assumed they were staying at the main house up on the hill.

Thomas Bennett had a huge white smile. "Great work," he said. "It was easier to catch him than we thought."

"Thomas, what's going on?" Janie asked.

"Stay out of it," he commanded.

"No. You always told me that no one would get hurt," she said.

"Shut her up," he told Frank.

Frank walked in front of us holding his gun with the long silencer in his right hand and with his left hand took a strong swing to slap Janie. I reached out and stopped his hand before he managed to hit her. She curled up even closer to me.

"Hold off," Thomas said. "Janie, you get my point? Just be quiet."

She nodded her head.

"What do we do with the bait?" Al asked. "We didn't even need her."

"Have them bring her in," Thomas Bennett said.

Al went to the door and said something and the next thing I knew Sharlee was being pushed through the door. Behind her were two guys I had seen before. They were in King-Fu's entourage the night we were at Brother's Club. In fact, I had decked one of them. They had big grins when they saw me.

Sharlee resisted but when she saw me she said, "Hank, what are they doing?"

"Shut up and sit down," Frank said.

I felt terrible that she was here. Frank pushed her to the coach just on my left.

"Why her?" I asked, already knowing the answer.

Al said, "I kept asking you to come to my party but you didn't show any interest. I saw how you kept looking at her the night we had dinner, so we thought we would use her as bait. It looks like we didn't need her."

"Did they hurt you?" I asked.

Sharlee said, "These two lowlifes were waiting at my house when I got back from dinner. Then they took me."

She didn't mention the name of Sam Oliver.

I looked at King-Fu's two guys. "And you were the one's who threw the firebomb into Clyde and Rochelle's house, right?"

Al laughed. "Anything to turn the pressure up. King-Fu's friends have been more than helpful."

Sharlee looked over at Janie curled up tight against my right side. Her face tightened.

Thomas Bennett looked around the room and said, "You two guys wait outside."

King-Fu's assistants turned and went out the back door.

"Frank, go pay them," Bennett said.

Frank carried his gun outside and a moment later I heard a "Pfaat, Pfaat" as the silencer muffled the sound of the gunshots, and then "Ahhhhh", as one was moaning and then another "Pfaat," and then it was quiet.

Janie crouched against me even tighter and let out a small moan. Sharlee sat up straight and I saw her eyes scanning the room. She's someone like me who grew up hearing the sounds of gunshots in the neighborhood. But I knew what she was feeling.

Frank came back in the room and resumed his place. Al chuckled, his large belly moving up and down. Burt stood to the side of Bennett his gun in ready position.

"So you want to own my startup company," I said, looking at Bennett.

"Just to be a partner," he said. "Only you're making it difficult."

"How'd you find out about the company?" I asked.

"Simple market research. You were featured in a trade journal a few weeks ago. We investigated and it was the perfect size and stage for us to invest in, and it represents a tremendous return on investment."

"Therefore, Janie appears on the scene," I stated.

Bennett laughed. "We've found this to be an extremely effective market research method to gain a better understanding of the strengths and weakness of our target, to get an inside look you might say."

Janie moaned, "I'm sorry Hank, really sorry. I tried to get out of it, but they threatened me."

"I know how they operate," I said to her. I turned back to Bennett. "That's how you knew about the fight with King-Fu, about Clyde and Rochelle, and about me going to the trade show in San Jose, and most important, where I kept all my company records so you could take them. She was going to your house in Beverly Hills each night to tell you all the details of what she learned."

"My, my," he said. "You certainly are perceptive and sneaky to know about the house in Beverly Hills. But, yes, Janie certainly did a good job although we had to significantly coach her hard to keep her in line."

"And all the other stuff, the lawsuit, the emotional jerking me around, was there to beat me down."

"My friend, let me give you some advice from a lawyer. It is better to negotiate with someone who is in a weak position than in a strong position. It is just part of the game."

"And now you own my company," I stated, "and give me the same treatment you gave to Robert Montet and Tina Bernardo."

"Who are they?" Janie whimpered.

I stated, "Robert Montet was assisted in a suicide, jumping off the Golden Gate Bridge, and Tina Bernardo was shot twice in the back. She worked for these guys."

Bennett said, "Robert Montet didn't sign the full agreement and started to cause trouble. It was necessary to protect our investment. Tina got greedy and we can't have any of that. If Robert had signed the full agreement none of that would have been necessary."

They were the greedy ones, four billion dollars worth and more companies in the pipeline. I needed to think quickly and to buy some time. "If I sign the agreement will you let them go?" I asked, nodding at Janie and Sharlee.

"Anything's negotiable," he said.

"Don't do it Hank," Sharlee said.

"Shut up fish bait," Frank said. He took a couple of steps forward and was an arms length away from Sharlee pointing the gun at her head.

She remained still, staring into his eyes.

"Let me pop her boss," he said waiving the long silencer back and forth at my face and then Sharlee's.

"Hold off," Al said.

Frank quit moving the gun but stood in a menacing position in front of Sharlee just off to my left.

She turned to me and said, "Don't sign it Hank."

"Will you let them go?" I asked, knowing Sharlee was absolutely right. They had just killed two guys and wouldn't let any of us go. Janie and Sharlee would end up like Tina Bernardo and I would be thrown off something tall.

"Sign the agreement and we can arrange it," Al said.

"Okay, I'll sign it, but let them go first."

Bennett laughed. "Sign it first."

"Okay."

Bennett runed to Burt and commanded, "Burt, go up to the house and get the contract. It's on my desk in the office."

Burt nodded and left and we waited. Frank continued to hold the gun in front of Sharlee's face.

"Hank, don't give in to these creeps," Sharlee said.

"It's okay," I said to her. "Just get out of here after I sign the agreement."

That seemed to relax Al, thinking he had won the war. "Well, it sure looks like we caught the rabbit," he said.

"The rabbit?" I asked.

"That's what we've been calling you. Look how you and Janie were behaving, going at it like rabbits."

Janie dropped her head. Sharlee looked at me with tight eyes.

Frank and Al started to laugh. Bennett showed his pearly white teeth in a creepy grin.

"Bet she's something else," Frank said turning to look at Al while slightly shifting the handgun away from Sharlee's face.

That was my moment. I sprang from the couch reaching out and grabbing his right wrist with my left hand while turning the long silencer barrel of the gun away from Sharlee. He managed to get off a shot that went into the wall next to the couch. He had strong arms and brought his left hand over and attempted to pry my hand off his wrist. His face was open, so with my right hand I discharged a smashing punch to his nose and he grunted. He was still trying to get the gun back into firing position but I continued to keep a hold on his wrist and with my right foot I unloaded a hard kick into his groin so hard that I felt him lift off the ground. He let out a deep grunt and dropped the gun and I quickly kicked it in the direction of Sharlee, while I got one hand on his chin and the other on the back of his head and I twisted his thick neck until something snapped. He went down with a thud.

Al was standing in front of us, frozen, his eyes wide. I quickly went over to him and delivered a crashing blow into his soft belly just under his heart. The wind went out of him and he dropped to his knees and started coughing.

Thomas Bennett was headed for the door and I sprinted and dove for his back and as he fell his face went through the glass window on the door and his body bounced back with my weight on him forcing him to the ground. I saw bloody skin hanging on shards of broken glass and then looked it his face. The skin was peeled back on his upper mouth which now had an opening twice its normal size. I quickly got off of him, stood up, and then stomped hard on his head. He passed out. In my anger I wanted to continue stomping in order to drive his soul into hell, but something else inside of me constrained me. Enough had been done. There was no need to release my anger in that way.

I turned and went back to Sharlee who was holding the gun and took it from her and I heard running outside as Burt came bursting through the door. It smashed into Bennett's bleeding face. Burt was surprised and it took him a moment to raise his gun. My Marine training came back and I fired twice hitting him both times in the chest and he dropped his gun and put his hands to his chest dropping to his knees next to Bennett. Burt made a feeble attempt to reach for the gun so I shot him directly in the heart and he fell forward and didn't move.

Al wheezed a couple of times and then he stopped breathing.

Janie started to cry, deep anxious sobs.

Sharlee looked at Janie and then at me and shook her head. "Rabbits," she said. Her eyes became moist.

EPILOGUE

Things moved fast after that. Besides some interviews with LAPD detectives, my life was consumed by work. About two weeks after the event in Malibu, Unipac approached me and made a buyout offer for TechZip.

On a Thursday morning Sam Oliver and Paul Kent flew down to Los Angeles to meet with Robert Campbell and me.

So there we were with the Chairman of the Board and the CEO of Unipac in this small conference room that was half filled with wires and odd pieces of computer parts. Sam and Paul seemed perfectly at ease in making an unbelievable offer. They proposed four hundred million dollars for TechZip, half in cash and half in shares in Unipac. When I did my MBA I read about deals like this, where substantial sums of money were paid for startup companies, ones having no real sales. It was the technology that mattered and ours was unique. No wonder BMP Capital wanted TechZip.

I was confused with Unipac's offer and didn't know what to do. Luckily Robert was there. He was an old hand at this kind of thing.

Something in me told me not to accept their offer. There was this internal pride at work that I could build TechZip on my own, but I knew that would be difficult. In actual fact, Unipac was a proven company with the infrastructure to turn our product into a commercial success.

Robert and I left the room to discuss their offer. He had experience with this kind of thing and advised that we should take the deal. We walked back into the room and Robert put a counter offer on the table which was immediately accepted by Sam and Paul. We ended up selling TechZip for five hundred million dollars, half in cash and half in shares in Unipac.

Twenty percent of the sale price went to Robert and the rest to me. There were several conditions and one of them was that I had to work for Unipac for at least one year to help with the transition. That seems to be normal with startup company buyouts.

On Friday, the day after our meeting, I drove my Jeep to San Jose where I checked into a hotel. On Saturday I bought a business suit and on Monday I walked into the Unipac Headquarters where I was given a temporary desk not far the desk of Sam Oliver.

The following weeks were a blur as I attended meetings, visited

Unipac factories and worked directly with the division that was taking over TechZip.

Sam Oliver was particularly kind to me. Several times he invited me to his house in Santa Cruz for Sunday lunch.

Sam's wife, Margaret, was extremely nice to me, and she reminded me of Rochelle. Maybe it was the Baptist background?

During those Sunday lunches they asked a lot of questions about me, so I told them things about growing up in Los Angeles, and my most recent experience with BMP Capital.

★ ★ ★

I had to fly to Los Angeles to be a witness in the court trial of the State of California against BMP Capital. It lasted two days and in the end BMP Capital was ruled guilty. An accounting firm was assigned to recuperate all assets held by the company and distribute them to the harmed entrepreneurs. I was glad that Mrs. Montet would at least be getting something, although that would never make up for the loss of her son.

I saw Sharlee and Janie at the trial, but they both avoided me. I understood why. At the trial I learned that Janie had transferred her university credits to San Diego State University where she was attending classes.

During that trip I visited Clyde and Rachelle and arranged to have their house completely remodeled because of the fire. I offered to buy them a bigger house in a safer neighborhood, but they refused. Rochelle said, "This is where God has put me," so I let it go at that. You don't argue with Rochelle.

Rochelle told me that Sharlee now had a job working with Los Angeles County Social Services. I was glad for her, as that's what she always wanted to do. When I saw her at the trial my heart longed for her and I wanted to talk with her, but there just wasn't an opportunity. She came at her appointed time, testified, and left. I tried to call her several times and sent emails, but no answers. I completely understand that I hurt her and it must have been terrifying to see what I did to Al, Frank and Burt.

At the trial I spoke with Detective Curly Grady, who informed me that he left the LAPD. He was now an independent detective working as an investigator for some very large insurance companies. He told me he was making a lot more money than with the LAPD, and he was glad to be out from under the thumb of his "Femi-Nazi supervisor".

I hired Detective Grady to help me with something. I want to find my real father, who was last known to be in Louisiana. Grady recently told me that he is making progress and has found some leads.

One of the most unsettling things at the trial was to see the lawyer Thomas Bennett. His once handsome face was now distorted and because of all the scar lines it seemed like his face was made up of large fish scales.

When he saw me he stared at me with a look of evil and revenge. I've seen some tough stares from people in the neighborhoods where I grew up, but this one from Bennett troubled me. It gave me shivers and told me to watch my back.

Thomas Bennett hired some of the best lawyers in Los Angeles and it looked like all charges against him would be dropped. He had convincingly distanced himself from the company and even made himself look like a victim. He claimed that BMP Capital was just a minor client and he had only offered them legal advice. There was no trace of ownership of Bennett to BMP Capital, as the company was owned by a complex web of offshore companies and it was therefore impossible to identify the real owners. So, there was nothing on paper that connected Bennett with the company.

I understood that my testimony against Bennett was weak, as there was no conclusive evidence. Bennett was a master at covering his tracks.

At the trial I found out that Bennett had law offices in London and Frankfurt, so it made me wonder if he was doing the same thing in Europe.

I definitely will stay cautious because of that guy.

As far as what I did to Frank, Burt and Al Mancini I guess I should have feelings of regret. Honestly I don't. That's just part of my emotional makeup. I still scare myself sometimes because of the deep down anger I carry. Maybe I'm getting better.

* * *

Most recently, Sam Oliver asked me to accompany him on a trip to Europe. One shocking thing that recently happened was that an old friend of his, Pete Vine, was killed in an airplane crash in the Mediterranean. They never found the plane. Mr. Vine had been the majority owner in Vine Industries, a major international conglomerate.

With the death of Mr. Vine, the share price of Vine Industry fell and it turned out that the Board at Vine Industries made a strange decision to sell off the company.

Sam told me that Unipac bought a number of the businesses of Vine Industries and he wanted to visit one of their factories in Barcelona that Unipac was considering to buy. He said that the factory made advanced bar code readers and it might be a good place to set up TechZip. He wanted me to come along to help with the evaluation.

The thought of a trip to Europe was of interest me in that I always wanted to go to Paris to visit the Orsay Museum. In my apartment in Venice Beach I had a cheapo poster reproduction of a painting by Jean-François Millet titled, *The Angelus*. It was destroyed in the fire.

I used to look at that painting every day and promise myself that someday I would go see the original. Now's my chance. It's a simple painting, a man and a woman standing in a field at the end of the day, their heads bowed, praying.

That thought pleases me. That's how it should be at the end of a day. In the painting, on the horizon one sees a church tower. It is a reinforcing symbol that seems to support the couple. The man and woman remind me of Clyde and Rochelle.

That's how I want to be.

AUTHOR'S NOTE

Through personal experience I got the idea to write Startup which is the first book in the Blue Fate series. Some years ago I sold a company that I had started and afterwards one story idea got stuck in my mind. What would happen if an evil venture capital company went around stealing companies? And, what methods might they use?

To bring life to the story I needed a main character that was vulnerable, and Hank Morgan was created. He is someone who has had the deck stacked against him. He grew up without a mother and father, was shuffled through foster homes, and learned to survive on the mean-streets of Los Angeles. Because of this he is unable to experience a full set of normal human emotions. Anger is at the forefront of his emotions, at least when he is being aggressed. Indeed he is a flawed character. His culture and experiences have a lot to do with who he is. At the same time, Hank is someone who inherently wants to do the right thing. Yet, he makes choices that lead him toward personal pain. In seeking love he becomes infatuated with the wrong woman and from that point on is confronted by a set of forces that are out to take away everything he owns.

The question is whether Hank is bound by his past or can he rise above it? This leads to a broader question. Can people break free from negative constraints found in their culture and upbringing? If not, do we just accept that we are bound by the environment in which we live?

Another observation is that Hank is the antithesis of the idealized perfection found in our modern world. We are taught to expect perfect lovers, perfect marriages, perfect children, perfect churches, perfect pastors, perfect employees and perfect politicians. But in reality human nature consists of a conflicting mix of human nobility and cruelty, of self-giving versus greed. And that's what is found in Startup where even the good guys are flawed. At the same time, the antagonists in the story are very evil characters who use any means possible to steal other people's assets.

Hank makes choices to do the right thing in spite of his emotional limitations. At the end of the book his entrepreneurial idea is successful and he ends up joining the Unipac Corporation. From California Hank travels to Spain with Sam Oliver, the Chairman of Unipac, and the adventures continue.

In the following books, Sam Oliver will attempt to unravel this mystery of who is attacking them. Hank Morgan will take a minor role as some new characters are introduced, but he will appear as the lead character in a future books. Of the new characters, one will be confronted by an extremely unusual moral dilemma. And then the conflict deepens.

Therefore, in reading the Blue Fate series, what may seem simple in the beginning is in fact shrouded by obscurity. Isn't that how it is sometimes? The simplicity by which we interpret things is in fact only a beginning and there is deeper significance in events and circumstances.

One definition of wisdom is, 'the power of true and just discernment'. Even though we think we may perceive things correctly, in fact do we discern them as they really are? If fate throws difficulty at us, do we really think about and understand the causes? Do we just suffer and go along with whatever is handed to us? Or, can we make wise choices to overcome difficult circumstances and better navigate through the world? I invite you to join me in the Blue Fate series as the plot expands and more characters are sucked into fate's vortex.

Cass Tell
Costa Brava, Spain

Your opinion is important to me!

I hope you enjoyed my book and I'd love to receive your feedback.
As the book is still fresh in your mind, please leave some comments
or a review on any of the following websites:

Amazon — www.amazon.com
Barnes & Noble — www.barnesandnoble.com
Goodreads — www.goodreads.com

And I invite you to visit my website www.casstell.com to find out
more details about all books in the Blue Fate series and my other
books.

Thank you!